Leaving Traces

Janet Lee

Contents

Chapter One: Blood Tests

- -

Chapter One: Blood Tests

Vvvt. Vvvt.

I glance down at my phone and shriek when I see a very inappropriate picture of my husband on the screen. I slam my hand down to cover it.

"What?" Mom asks with a laugh. I snatch my phone off the counter and laugh nervously.

"Nothing." I say. My parents are here, my brothers, Alice, Zane's parents and Aunt Mia, Vanessa, Colton...everyone except for Zane. "I have to pee." I say, and I really do. I get up and leave the dinner table, rushing off to the bathroom. As I sit on the toilet, I open the message and see a picture of Zane completely naked, hard, gripping his erection and biting his lip.

This fucking man.

I put my phone on the counter and finish my business, and then I flush and wash my hands, grabbing my phone again.

Me: I'M AT DINNER WITH THE WHOLE FAMILY

Hubby: SEND NUDES

Me: HORN DOG!!!!

Hubby: JUST SEND A TITTY

Ever since Lucas, I've never sent a nude. Now, after being married for two years, I still have never sent another nude. It's not that I don't trust Zane, but he's on an NFL team. If any one of the guys gets ahold of his phone...

Me: no

Hubby: Rosie, I'm not going to send it to anybody

Me: I know. But no

Hubby: okay

I feel guilty. I put the picture in my vault app and slip out of the bathroom.

"Are you okay?" Mom asks.

"Yeah, are you like, pregnant or something?" Alice asks hopefully. I laugh.

"Alice, I'm not pregnant."

Every single time I come over here, if I do anything remotely showing a pregnancy symptom, like put my hand on my stomach, go pee, or admit I'm tired, Alice will ask if I'm pregnant. The whole family has been wondering when Zane and I were going to have children.

We go back to dinner and I tune everyone out.

We've been married two years. He proposed in June and we got married in October. I would see him every single day at work and after work he would go to football practice. A few months before NFL season was supposed to start, the quarterback for the Packer's announced he was retiring. At tryouts, Zane blew everything out of the water, and even though he didn't go to college for football, he was first choice for the new quarterback. America was skeptical of him at first, but after the first game, there was no hesitation about Alexander Caulton.

My husband took his team to the Super Bowl, and the game is this Sunday. Our whole family is flying out and sitting in the VIP section, and I can't wait. I'm so proud to support him the way he supported me.

I'm twenty nine now, and Zane is thirty. Finn is thirty one and Tanner is thirty three. Little Alice is twelve, nearly thirteen. Zane relented custody of her about a year ago, mostly because she asked but partially because every time we tried to have sex, we were interrupted.

Since he got added to the team in July and the season started in September, he has spent most of his time since July away from home, either in Green Bay for practice or traveling the country for games. Since July I've seen him once a week, and since September I've seen him on Thanksgiving, Christmas Eve, Christmas Day, New Years Eve, and New Years Day. That's it.

I miss him so much, and in our free time on those days, we were having sex, because the desire for each other gets pent up.

Sunday though, he's free until August and I can't wait.

When we finish with dinner and everything is clean, I settle down on the couch for a movie with our family.

I seat myself between Alice and Madison. My phone vibrates again, but it's not Zane this time. It's instagram.

lost_reagan has sent you a message!

Frowning, I unlock my phone and click on the notification.

lost_reagan: can you give me your number I need to talk to you

What the hell?

Me: uh, who are you?

lost_reagan: my name is Reagan I promise I'm not crazy, just please give me your number so I can call you

Me: I'm married.

lost_reagan: I know I saw in your bio

Me: no you can't have my number

lost_reagan: then let me meet you somewhere

Me: you're crazy! I'm blocking you.

lost_reagan: no! Please! I'm not crazy! Belle, you have to listen to me. Please.

Is this guy insane?

lost_reagan: I'm not crazy, I swear

Me: fine. But I'm not giving you my number. I'll meet you somewhere.

lost_reagan: okay your house?

Me: no. Wtf

Me: hold on

I think hard, and then I Google something.

Me: meet me at 7335 W Good Hope Rd, 100, Milwaukee, WI 53223 in thirty minutes.

lost_reagan: okay

With my heart beating violently, I stand up.

"I'm kinda tired. I'm gonna go." I say.

"Alright, drive safe." Mom says. Everyone hugs me goodbye, and I clip Tank's leash on and walk off to my midnight blue Chevy Suburban.

I get in and start the drive to the Starbucks.

I get there in twenty minutes.

Right when I put the car in park, my phone vibrates.

Madison: I saw your phone screen and I'm not going to judge. If you need me to save you, let me know, ok? I won't tell anyone.

Me: thank you

I get out with Tank and lean against the hood of my car, waiting.

After a few minutes, somebody near me clears their throat.

I look up to lock eyes with chocolate brown eyes. The man before me looks my age with wavy brown hair.

He looks me up and down for a minute.

"Reagan?" I ask. His eyes snap up to meet mine.

"Yes." He sticks his hand out. "Reagan Theo Johnson."

"Rosabelle Caulton." I say awkwardly shaking his hand. Tank starts sniffing him, and then he sits in front of me. "So...I know you didn't message me for no reason, Reagan."

"I don't know how to tell you this." He hesitates. "But I think you're my sister."

My eyebrows shoot up.

"Your sister?" I laugh. "No. That's impossible."

"Well I know Theo is a family name. Every guy in your family has that middle name." He stuffs his hands in his pockets.

He's not wrong.

"So? A lot of people have the same Theo."

"We have the same hair, same eye shape and color, same nose, same lips..." he trails off.

"A lot of people-"

"And my birthday is June twelfth."

That makes me so silent, staring at him.

He's taller than me by maybe two inches, but he's not wrong. Our features are so similar, we look like we could be siblings.

"Your birthday is June twelfth?" I whisper.

"Yes."

And my birthday is June twelfth.

"No." I say finally. "My twin died."

At that, he looks away.

"That's what they told you?" He asks softly.

"What time were you born?" I ask.

"Two in the morning. Some time in there, I don't know the exact minute."

I hop up onto the hood of my car.

"Reagan..." I shake my head.

"Look." He digs into his wallet and pulls out a photo.

The photo is of my Mom, holding two babies. One is wrapped in a pink blanket, and one is wrapped in a blue blanket. She looks tired, and she has tears on her cheeks.

Reagan and Rosabelle. Rosabelle and Reagan.

"Where did you get this?" I ask.

"From my Mom." He sighs. "My adopted mother."

Adopted.

I take a photograph of the picture and hand it back to him, and then I hop off the hood of my car, stumbling slightly. He grabs my arms to steady me, and I clear my throat.

"Get in the car."

"Where are we going?" He asks.

"The hospital." I reply. "To get a blood test."

He doesn't protest at all.

After sitting awkwardly beside my supposed brother in the waiting room for three hours, the doctor who took our blood comes walking in. He gestures for us to follow him.

He heads us to a room in the back, and I sit down on the hospital bed. Reagan leans against it and waits.

"You two are definitely related." He says when he shuts the door. "And given by your birthdays and your medical records, Reagan, you were born on June twelfth at 2:23AM and Rosabelle, you were born on June twelfth at 2:26AM. The chance that you are twins is very likely." He clears his throat. "Rosabelle, I have to ask you something personal. Do I mind if I ask in front of Reagan here?"

I squirm slightly.

"You can ask." I mumble.

"Are you sexually active?"

"Um...yeah."

He nods slowly, flipping through the test.

"Your HCG levels are extremely high. You are pregnant, and you might have more than one baby."

Pregnant? I'm pregnant?

More than one baby?

"And judging by the look on your face, I'm going to guess you didn't know. Congratulations."

He hands us papers.

"You guys can leave at any time."

He walks out, and the door clicks shut behind him.

Okay, first of all, my twin brother isn't dead, he's sitting right next to me, and second, I'm pregnant?

"Are you okay?"

My eyes snap up to meet Reagan's.

"I'm pregnant."

"Yes. Are you happy?"

"I-" I cut off. "Yeah."

He pauses. "It is your husbands baby, right?"

Chapter Two: FaceTime

- -

Chapter Two: FaceTime

I turn slightly in the mirror, running my hand over my belly.

There is a tiny little bump there, one so small you wouldn't notice unless you were looking. When I lie down, it sticks out much more. I just thought I was gaining weight.

My breasts have been sore, but I figured I was just going to start my period. My period hasn't come in a few months, but it's always been irregular, so I thought nothing of it.

This is why I've been so tired and nauseous in the mornings.

This is why certain scents make me want to throw up.

This is why I pee once every two hours.

So many questions run through my mind.

How far along am I?

Is the baby healthy?

Was the doctor right? Am I having twins?

Why did my parents tell me Reagan died in the womb?

Are Zane and I ready for this kind of commitment? A baby?

A baby. Maybe even two. A smile breaks out on my lips.

We're gonna have a baby. A little tiny baby, that our love created.

It's growing inside of me.

When do I tell Zane?

If I tell him now, it could affect him playing at the Super Bowl, and it's his dream to take his team for the win. It's only three days.

It's Thursday night and we fly out there tomorrow, but I need to wait until after the game to tell Zane the news.

Deciding this is the best for me, I go downstairs to the living room and turn on the TV.

I love our house. It's worth 1.2 million dollars. It has eight bedrooms, six full bathrooms and two half's. There is also five fireplaces, a rec room in the basement, a two car garage, three living rooms, a study that we made into a movie theatre, another study in our bedroom, two breakfast areas, a formal dining room, and five acres of land.

I worship this house so much. It's my sanctuary.

I think back to the last time Zane went inside of me without a condom, and the only time that rings a bell is Thanksgiving Day, he went in raw that night because it was the first time we had sex since September fifth. We were going to get the pill but I can't remember if we ever did.

Conception can be anywhere from a few hours to five days after sex.

We went to sleep that night and I went and got the pill the next morning.

If you're already pregnant, the pill won't do anything.

I think of my symptoms and sigh.

How did I not know sooner?

I have had weird cravings, nausea that usually leads to throwing up, dizziness, tiredness, sore and swollen breasts, headaches, mood swings, and heartburn.

I just never really pieced it together. With gymnastics, I was always sore, and I do gymnastics lightly now and I go with Alice all the time and help her on the side.

The doctor said my HCG levels are high, but from everything I looked up, that said it can mean nothing.

But it doesn't feel like nothing. My gut is telling me I'm having twins.

My mind wanders to my brother and I frown.

Does Reagan feel abandoned by my parents? Why did they tell me he died? Who raised my brother? Is twin telepathy real?

Maybe it's only real with identical twins.

My phone starts ringing though, grabbing my attention completely. It's already ten, so I know what time it is. Smiling, I drop my shirt and swipe to answer.

If only Zane knew how different things are now. I want to tell him to exciting news, but I want to tell him in person. I wonder if he's going to be the kind of husband that whispers to my belly and kisses it and rubs it.

When we called last night, we talked about everything, from when we start our family to if we're going to build a swimming pool or not.

Who knew I was already pregnant.

When the word connecting on FaceTime disappears and I see my husbands handsome face, I smile.

"Hi baby!" He exclaims. "I miss you." He grins.

"I miss you too." I smile, climbing into bed. Tank comes running at the sound of Zane's voice, pounding onto the bed. I turn the camera to show him to Zane.

"Tank!" Zane exclaims. Tank whines loudly and licks the screen. I laugh and wipe it off, turning the camera back to me. "I love you guys." He pouts. "I can't wait to come home! I can't wait until tomorrow Rosie, I get to see my baby!"

"I know!" I exclaim. "I'm going to your hotel, right?"

"Yes." He nods. "But I'll be at practice. Go to the front desk and tell them you're my wife and that you need a key. They know you're coming. I'll be done around five, and then I'll come see you, okay?"

"Okay." I smile.

"Rosie, I need to talk to you about something, and I was going to wait but I don't want to wait anymore. I want to talk about it now."

"Okay." I frown, shifting slightly on the bed.

"When I get home...I want to start our family."

My eyebrows raise.

"You mean you want to impregnate me?" I ask.

"Yes. You know, we could do it tomorrow. Or start tomorrow, I mean...if you want." His phone is resting on something, so he starts messing with his fingers. "Do you want to Rosie?

I want to tell him so badly, but I don't want to do it over the phone.

"Rose?" He asks.

"What? Yes, we can start our family."

He grins.

"Really?" He asks. "You mean it?"

"Of course I mean it." I smile.

"Oh my gosh baby girl, I can't wait. We're going to have seven boys and one girl."

"Zane, I told you we're not having eight children!"

"Why not?" He whines.

"Because I don't want my body to break!" I laugh.

"Five?" He asks softly.

"We'll see." I say.

"Can guys do gymnastics?" He asks suddenly.

"Yes." I nod.

"Well...well then our kids will do sports. They don't have to do football or gymnastics, but they have to do something. And our boys? They're going to be raised to open doors and treat women with respect. I'm not raising a little prick. And our girls? They're going to learn how to be polite, just like their Mommy...but they're going to be confident, because lets face it, with genes like mine, they're bound to look like sex gods."

I laugh softly.

"Gosh, I miss you baby."I murmur.

"I miss you too Rosie." He smiles. "In twenty four hours, right now..." he looks at his watch. "We'll probably be having sex or cuddling."

"I know." I laugh.

He pauses, and then his smile fades and he frowns.

"Rose?"

"Yes?" I ask.

"I just would like to apologize for asking for nudes earlier. I wasn't trying to make you uncomfortable, I just...I want you, Rosie, and I'm having a hard time dealing with the fact that I can't have you."

"I know baby, it's okay." I smile.

"Okay."

We fall into a comfortable silence.

"Want me to flash a titty?" I grin. His eyes widen slightly.

"Are you serious?" He asks. I nod, and he nods his head rapidly.

I set the camera up and then grab the hem of his shirt and lift it up all the way. I hear him gasp, and then there's a pause.

"I'm gonna go masturbate, I'll call you back." He says, rushed. The line clicks.

Chuckling, I slip under the covers and set my alarm to get up at five tomorrow, and then I shift slightly in bed, rest my hand on my tiny belly. I can't wait until I'm bigger, until the baby is born. I'm so excited. Yawning, I settle deeper into the pillow and close my eyes. I fall into a deep sleep with dreams about babies and Zane.

———

This is a shorter chapter but really cute and made me miss Zane a lotVote and comment ~Sam

Chapter Three: Text Message

C hapter Three: Text Message

I sit in the hotel room in Dallas, my stomach churning. My nausea has been horrible all day. I woke up and ran straight for the bathroom, and the plane ride was spent with me breathing in a bag.

When the plane landed, I quietly told the flight attendant I was pregnant and I needed off the plane, and she let me be the first one off.

I ran straight to the bathroom and threw up.

On the bus to the hotel, I kept my head against the window and had to keep breathing into a bag.

Now I'm finally in the hotel in Zane's room, and I'm ripping through his suitcase looking for a pair of clear clothes.

None. He hasn't done any laundry.

I find myself smiling as I zip up his suitcase and search the room for any spare laundry. I grab my wallet and and the room key and slip out of the room, onto the elevator.

I bring his whole suitcase downstairs and into the laundry room, popping some money into the machine. I put all of his clothes in the wash and get some detergent, and then I sit back as the wash works.

My phone vibrates.

Hubby: are you here yet

Me: yes I'm doing your laundry. You didn't have any clean clothes

Hubby: you were in my suitcase?

Me: yeah

Hubby: you should come to the stadium

Me: your wash is in the wash

Hubby: :(

Me: I'll come when it's finish but how do I get in

Hubby: I'll send someone. Bring everyone it'll be fun

I don't want to go at all. I feel horrible and I want to go to bed, but it's for my baby, and I've missed him so much.

Me: alright

Three hours later the bus was rolling to a stop in front of the stadium. I text Zane the moment we're standing outside.

Me: we're here

I'm so excited to see him. We move closer to the doors and I see the message go to read, and then he doesn't reply.

Nauseous, I lean against the wall of the building.

"Belle, are you alright?" Vanessa asks. "You look miserable."

"She's right sweetheart." Mom puts her hand on my forehead. "Are you okay?"

"I'm fine." I wave them off, although I'm feeling slightly dizzy.

Madison walks over to me and grabs my wrist to check my pulse.

"Belle, your heart is pounding." She says calmly.

"I'm fine." I insist.

The door to the stadium is thrown open and a random guy comes walking over to us.

"You guys are Alex's family?" He asks. We all nod, and he nods towards the stadium doors.

We all start to walk, and we reach a flight of stairs and my entire body tells me not to go up the stairs, but I do it anyways.

When we reach the top, I'm sweating.

He brings us to stadium seats where the Packers are on the field, and my eyes search for number ten. I see Zane in his helmet, and we all settle down to watch. Vanessa sits on my left and Mom sits on my right.

Exhausted, I rest my head on my Mom's shoulder and shut my eyes.

"She just fell asleep?" I hear a soft voice ask.

"Yeah. I think she's coming down with something sweetheart, she's been looking sick all day." Another voice replies. I shift my head on the warm vanilla and mint scent. I can feel the warmth radiating off of the body, and I'm moving, but I'm not walking.

"Sick how?" The voice continues. "Flu?"

"I don't know. Maybe."

I recognize the other voice as a female, but the voice that belongs to the person holding me is male.

"Maybe she should go to the doctor." The male says. "What time was your flight again?"

"Seven, but we met at the airport at five."

"She went to bed around ten fifteen." The male says.

Only one person could know...

My head snaps up, slamming against the chin of my husband. His hair is damp from a shower and he's wearing a black long sleeve polo and jeans. He smells just like home. My legs are around is waist, my head on his shoulder.

Did I fall asleep? How? Where? On who?

God, I really don't feel good.

"Hi baby girl." Zane grins down at me, and my heart floods with warmth and happiness.

"Hi." I murmur. I wrap my arms around his neck and hug him. He stops walking to hug me back, and then sets me on the ground.

The moment my feet hit the floor, the world starts spinning. We're outside of the stadium again, walking towards the bus. The sun is setting, the sky random colored of blues and purples and yellows and oranges. It was warm outside earlier, but now it's chilly. I feel Zane's hands gripping my shoulders.

"Are you okay?" He asks.

"Yes." I lie.

I can't tell everyone I'm having issues because I'm pregnant.

"Maybe you need to eat." Madison says.

"Yeah, Madison is right." Mom says firmly. "Did you eat before you met us at the airport this morning?"

I pause.

"No..."

"And all we had was McDonald's when the plane landed at one." Mom sighs.

"You most definitely need to eat." Zane says. "Let's go to dinner." He rubs my back gently and then slips his arm around my shoulder. We start walking, but I pause again to hug him. He's so warm and cuddling. He chuckles lightly and wraps his arms around me, walking me backwards towards the bus. I struggle to keep up with him, and then I just place my feet on his feet and let him walk for the both of us.

We load up in the bus and I get the seat with Zane, my head against his shoulder.

After a half hour in the car, we stop at Applebees and Zane helps me inside and into the large booth. I'm in the outside seat thankfully, and our family squeezes in all around us.

"Are you on your period sweetheart?" Mom asks.

"I have some midol." Vanessa adds.

"No, I'm fine." I wave them off.

The waitress hands us the menus and takes our drink orders. I just got water. I feel so faint.

Zane kisses my forehead and my cheek softly as we wait for our drinks.

"You're sweating." He murmurs, removing my coat.

I really don't feel good. I'm especially nauseous.

"I'm going to go to the restroom." I say softly. I stand up and walk across the restaurant to the bathroom. I rush into a stall and throw up , gagging and spitting on bile. When I stop, I start dry heaving, and then I pause and start again.

Gosh, what is going on?

I flush the toilet when I'm certain I'm done, and I rinse my mouth and wash my hands.

"Are you okay sweetie?" An older woman asks. I glance at her.

"Yes." I mumble. "I'm pregnant."

Her eyes move to my left hand and she smiles.

"Congratulations." She smiles.

"Thank you." I smile back.

I'm still slightly queasy, so I stick around for a few more minutes.

When I'm certain I'm not going to vomit again, I push open the door to the bathroom.

Zane is earning calmly against the wall across from the restroom, an un-readable expression on his face.

"Do you have a mint?" I ask, already knowing the answer. He digs into his pocket and drops a wrapped mint in my hand. It's the kind that melts in your mouth. I pop it in my mouth and study him. He's here for a reason.

"I need to have a word with you." He says calmly.

"Okay..." I trail off.

"I wasn't trying to snoop, Rosie, but your phone lit up and I saw the messages."

He hands me my phone, and I press the power button.

Last night after we left the hospital, I gave Reagan my phone number, and I have a message from him.

Reagan: two questions. One, are you going to tell your husband about us? And two, are you going to tell him about the baby(ies)

Shit, this sounds bad, especially since I fell asleep before I had the opportunity to tell him about my twin.

"I'm not assuming anything." Zane says when I look up at him. "And I was not going through your phone. I trust you with my life. It lit and I saw the message. I've never heard of a Reagan before."

I glance over my shoulder at our watching family, shifting the mint in my mouth.

"Do you want to have this conversation now, or when we go back to the hotel?"

He hesitates.

"On a a scale of one to ten, ten being extremely serious, how serious is this?"

Telling him I'm not a twinless twin and that we're having a baby, maybe more than one?

"Three hundred." I decide. "And no, I'm not cheating on you."

"I didn't think you were. We can wait until we're alone. Let's go back to the table, our drinks are here and you look like you need some water."

I don't want to eat or drink anything in fear of throwing it up, but I walk with him to the table anyways.

We sit down at the table and I finish the mint and take small sips of water.

The waitress comes up to take our orders, and after they go around the table, she looks at me.

"I'm not hungry." I say truthfully.

"She's going to get a chicken Cesar salad." Zane says. I open my mouth to argue, but he gives me that strict husband look, telling me not to argue.

He's right almost every time anyways.

The waitress writes in her book.

"Grilled chicken?" She asks.

"Yes." Zane replies.

She collects the menus and leaves.

Since we got married, our relationship has changed a lot.

Before there was a lack of communication, which resulted in him leaving me after thinking I didn't care about Alice, but now we discuss everything, from how many ply toilet paper we're going to buy to what kind of car we drive. Communication is key, and we communicate well. Normally when something goes wrong, like one of us forgets to pay a bill, we don't examine who to blame, we examine how to fix the situation. He surprises me with little presents or back rubs or bubble baths, or he pops in when I'm working to give me coffee or food, and I return the favor. We support each other fully, and for the most part, we know what's best for each other. There isn't one task for one person. We do everything together. It's a team effort keeping the house clean.

We have a very strong, very happy marriage, and multiple ways to stay organized, like writing down our bank statements just in case something gets messed up, or a calendar on the fridge to remind us when to pay what bill and how much it is.

Last night when he left to masturbate, I fell asleep before I could tell him about Reagan. I feel guilty I didn't tell him right away, but I was just so tired.

I take small sips of my water and unlock my phone. I click on the notification from Reagan and text him back.

Me: you worded that as if we're messing around, Reagan

Reagan: i'm sorry

Me: I'm going to tell him

Reagan: let me know how it goes

———

I threw up two more times before we left the restaurant, and when we got to the hotel, I got right in the shower and put on his pajamas. I threw up in the shower too.

Standing in the bathroom, I brush my teeth and lift Zane's shirt to see if my belly grew.

It didn't, but it still. The bump is little enough for me to hide with clothes, but big enough that if somebody saw me naked, they would notice I have gained weight.

I walk out of the bathroom and into the hotel room itself. Zane is laying on the king size bed under the covers. The curtains are pulled shut, and the room is cold but it feels good.

"Are you ready to talk?" I ask softly. He grabs the remote and shuts off the TV. "I need you to understand I had every intention of telling you the first part last night, but I was tired and I fell asleep."

He nods slowly and waits for me to continue. "I was at my Mom's for dinner and your family was there too, and this guy named Reagan messages me on Instagram asking if he could call me. I told him I was married but he was insistent, so I left to meet him."

"You left to go meet with a stranger you met online?" He asks slowly.

"Yes." I sigh.

"Baby girl,"

"It was stupid, Zane. I know."

He just nods and signals for me to continue.

"When I got there, I met him." I grab my phone and go to instagram, finding a picture of Reagan. It shows his nose, lips, eyes, and hair perfectly. There's no mistaking that he's my brother. "And he told me that he's my twin brother."

Zane's jaw drops open and he sits up further, his eyes wide with curiosity.

"I told him he was full of it, you know? But we look alike."

"Yeah you do." He nods, studying the picture. "Same eye color and nose...and lips, and even your faces are shaped the same."

"Right, and I still didn't believe him because my parents wouldn't lie to me, but then he showed me this."

I grab my phone again, sitting down in front of him on the bed, my legs crossed. I show him the photo of my Mom holding me and Reagan as infants.

He studies it for a long time.

"Rosie..." he trails off.

"So we went to the hospital and got a DNA test, and we're siblings. His birthday is April twelfth and he's like...two or three minutes older than I am."

"Your parents lied." He murmurs. "But why?"

"I don't know." I whisper, messing with my hands. "All I know is he was adopted but he's an only child. His adopted Mom gave him the picture and he started searching for me. His middle name is Theo, Zane. I'm not a twinless twin."

"Well are you happy?" He asks.

"Yeah, but I'm mad at my parents. Nobody knows I went to see him though, except your Mom, but she doesn't know who I was going to see, she just knows I was going to see him. I guess she saw me texting him since I was sitting next to her."

He nods in understanding.

"Are you going to confront your parents?"

"Not yet." I shake my head. "I need to talk to Reagan first. I want you to meet him."

"Of course." He says, and he kisses the back of my hand.

We fall into a comfortable silence.

I need to tell him now. He saw the message of Reagan asking about the baby.

"Zane..." I begin slowly. "When I got blood work done...my hCG levels were really really high."

"What does that mean?" He murmurs.

"It means that I'm pregnant, and it might be more than one baby."

His eyes widen slightly.

"I figured you were pregnant when I saw the message, but more than one baby?" He whispers, his voice hushed. "We're gonna be parents?"

"We're gonna be parents." I smile.

He laughs in delight, leaning forward to kiss me softly.

"Oh my gosh baby, that's why you weren't feeling good?" He asks. "You should have told me! I would have brought you here to rest!"

"I didn't want to tell you until after the SuperBowl. I didn't want you to be distracted. I'm sorry you had to find out this way."

"It's okay." He grins widely. "So when I said I wanted to start a family last night, you knew?!"

"I knew." I nod. "I'm sorry."

"It's okay." He smiles brightly and kisses me again. "You lay down." He points to my pillow, and I don't argue. I lie down on my back, and he pulls my shirt up. "You know, last night when you flashed me, I knew your breasts were bigger."

I laugh softly and watch as he looks down at my belly.

"Rosie, do you already have a bump?"

"A tiny one." I nod. "I don't know anything about the pregnancy or the baby except for that I'm pregnant."

"Well we should go to the doctor. We could go right now."

"I really don't want to go anywhere else today." I admit quietly. "The morning sickness today is horrible. I spent the entire plane ride slipping into the bathroom to throw up. Every time I went to the bathroom at the restaurant, I was throwing up, and I threw up in the shower."

"Oh, baby." He murmurs. "I'm so sorry. You should get some sleep."

"I thought you wanted to have sex."

"I do, very badly, but you don't feel good right now. You're creating our child, or children. You get whatever you want."

He moves his head down to plant soft kisses on my belly.

"Hi baby." He whispers to my belly. He glances up at me with a smile. "I'm your Daddy." He reaches for my hands, linking his fingers through mine. "I'm not really sure if you hear me." He continues. "But I'm here, okay? Even if there's octuplets inside your Mommy, I'm here, and Mommy and I are so very excited to meet you guys. If you're a baby girl, you can go into the ballet, or gymnastics, or softball. Heck, you can do football if you want to. If you're a boy, you can do whatever you want too. You can go into baseball, or softball, or football, or gymnastics. Even if you want to do ballet, Mommy and I will love and support you. Did your know that your Mommy-gosh, she's so brilliant-she is the number one gymnast in the whole entire world? Yup, that's right. For another year or so, she's number one. She's brilliant. I hope you're okay in there. I'm not sure if you can see anything or whatever, so I'm going to cover Mommy up, just in case it's too bright in there and you're trying to sleep." He puts both hands on my stomach and places gentle kisses all over it. "Okay? Mommy and Daddy love you, or however many of you there are. I'm going to go now because Mommy is really not feeling good, and she needs to get some sleep."

He kisses my belly again and pulls the covers over me. It's only eight thirty as he turns off the light. He's in his underwear. I turn on my side and nuzzle into his side, taking in his homey scent.

"I love you." I mumble.

"I love you too." He whispers.

My head rests comfortably in the crook of his arm, and I can feel him drawing patterns on my arm.

"When should we tell our families?"

He takes a deep breath, and I love that I can hear it.

"When we know how far along you are can decide that." He murmurs. "I'm going to see if we can go to the doctor tomorrow." He adds.

I yawn, nodding my head slowly.

"Alright. I'm going to sleep now."

"Okay. I love you, baby girl."

I smile, shifting to be closer to him. I throw my leg over his body and nuzzle m nose into his side, my left arm reaching across him to grip his other side.

"I love you too." I murmur. I kiss his bare skin and slide my eyes shut.

———

Zane is so cute talking to the baby(ies) like that~Sam

Chapter Four: Ultrasound

ALEXANDER CAULTON ON THE SIDE EVERYONE AND HE IS PERFECT (SEAN O'PRY)Okay I'm done but seriously he's so attractive

———

Chapter Four: Ultrasound

I lie on the bed at the doctors office. Zane got out of practice and we told our families we were going to the store.

"So your hCG level was high?" The doctor asks. I'm really nervous for some reason. I'm clutching Zane's hand closely.

"Yeah, the doctor that told me said it might be twins."

She nods slowly and grabs a bottle of gel.

"And this is your first appointment?"

"Yes." I nod nervously.

"Well just to let you guys know, some people have naturally high hCG levels. It could mean that you aren't having twins. Are you having any symptoms?"

"Um, morning sickness...dizziness, heartburn...my period didn't come, but it's always irregular, my breasts aching..." I trail off.

"Alright. I'm going to put the gel on your stomach, and it's going to be cold."

I take a deep breath and nod anxiously, waiting. She pours the goo and turns on a monitor, and grabs the wand, putting it against my belly. She moves it around until she finds my uterus, and then she stops.

It looks all black in there. Am I not pregnant?

Oh my god, I'm not pregnant. My hand on Zane's loosens slightly, but she moves the wand again and a little blob appears on the monitor.

"There's your baby." She smiles. "It does look like it's only one though." She clears her throat and moves the wand a little bit. "The baby looks healthy." She adds. Zane kisses my forehead with a big smile on his face. I'm grinning too. "Let's see if we can find a heartbeat..." she moves it around a tiny bit, and pauses on one spot, turning up the volume. I hear the warping heartbeat come through the speaker, and my eyes fill with tears, but then I f rown.

While there is a heartbeat, it sounds...weird.

"Why does it sound like that?" Zane asks.

The doctor looks a little puzzled herself.

"It sounds like..." she pauses, moving the wand lower. The baby disappears, and a moment later, another one appears. "It was two heartbeats." She laughs. "You're having twins."

Twins, two little babies.

"And it looks like you have one placenta, which means that they're identical. That also means you're getting either two girls or two boys, because you can't have a boy and a girl that are identical."

Oh my god I'm so excited. Happy tears roll down my cheeks.

"Both of the babies are very healthy. Judging by your weight and your belly, along with the size of the babies, I'm going to say you're about eleven weeks along. Do you know of a time that you guys had sex that this could have happened?"

I pause, thinking.

"Thanksgiving." Zane nods.

She nods to herself.

"Alright. You said your period is irregular?"

"I'm an athlete." I explain. "It's always been irregular. Some months I get it, sometimes I don't get it for three months."

She nods in understanding, studying the babies. She moves the doppler so we can see both of the babies at once.

"I imagine you guys want this printed?"

"Yes." Zane and I say in sync. "Can you print out three of them please?"

She nods, freezing the picture of the twins on the screen. She prints them out and wipes off my belly. I sit up and pull my shirt down when she's done, and we all sit there studying the babies. She starts pointing out the head and the legs and feet and the arms.

"I'm going to say you're due in August, given the conception time. August nineteenth." She pauses. "That's the forty week mark, but because you're having twins, you will most likely give birth between July twenty ninth and August nineteenth. Strive to not given birth until August fifth, because thirty eight weeks is full term with twins." She pauses. "Now your symptoms of going to be much worse, as I'm sure you already know. The only thing I can tell you is that prenatal vitamins are not a joke. Make sure to eat well, three full meals a day, and if you're feeling nauseous, munching on crackers or something small like that can make you feel better. And also, listen to your body. If you feel like you need to sit down, do it. If you need to sleep, do it. You're pregnant. You have three beating hearts inside of yo ur body right now."

"Okay." I nod excitedly. "So tomorrow is twelve weeks, right?"

"Yes. Tomorrow is the second trimester."

I smile happily. She gives us our papers.

"Now, if finances are an issue, we have places that can help.

"Finances are not a problem." Zane says, kissing my hand.

"Okay. Do you want genetic testing to make sure the babies don't have any genetic diseases or birth defects? This test can also tell us whether or not there is a Y chromosome. If there is, you're having identical twin boys."

"Um..." I swallow. "What do you recommend?" I look at Zane and he nods in agreement with me.

"Well I usually tell people yes." She says. "But you have to understand that I will have to remove a small piece of your placenta, and there is a small chance that it can induce a miscarriage."

"Absolutely not." I say.

"I agree." Zane says. "I was born healthy and so was my sister. My wife was born healthy, as was her twin brothers and her older brothers. I see no reason our children would have anything wrong with them. We can find out the gender safely and at a later date."

"Exactly." I say, squeezing Zane's hand.

"Very well." She says. "Here are your pictures." She hands the photos of the twins to me. I stand up from the bed, lowering my shirt fully.

We go out to the lobby, my hand in Zane's, and we pay for the appointment, and then Zane pulls me outside and stops me.

"We're having twins!" He exclaims.

"We're having twins!" I cheer. He lifts me into a tight but gentle embrace, kissing me passionately.

"We should tell everyone." I say. "Tomorrow is the second trimester. We can tell them."

"Good idea." He says. "That way I can make sure you're taken care of while I'm on the field."

———

Two hours later, around eight at night, I'm sitting at the restaurant with our family, waiting impatiently for out food. I'm starving.

I glance at Zane and see him looking at me. His eyes wander around to our family and back to me, and then he raises both of his eyebrows.

I'm not good at delivering news, especially news this big. When I was announcing Zane and I were getting married, I just slammed the ring down on the dinner table. Shrugging, I pull out the picture of the ultrasound, stand up, and slam it down on the table with a loud slap. Everyone gives me confused looks and then they look at what I put down.

"No!" Vanessa gasps. "You're pregnant?!"

Everyone reaches for the picture at once, but Zane grabs it first.

"Pass it around the table before you guys start a fight." He chuckles.

"Twins?" Colton smiles, looking at his best friend.

"Twins." Zane nods with a grin.

Everyone looks happy, but Mom and Madison get all tears eyed.

When the photo reaches me again, everyone looks at me.

"How are you feeling?"

"So that's why you didn't feel good yesterday."

"How far along are you?"

"Are the twins healthy?"

"I hope they're identical."

"How will you tell them apart if they are identical?"

"They're healthy, right?"

"How far along are you again?"

"When did you find out?"

"How did you find out?"

"Okay, okay." I laugh, putting my hands up. "Tomorrow is twelve weeks. They're healthy, are are identical, I have absolutely no idea how we're going to tell them apart, they are identical, I found out on Thursday night, and I found out from a blood test."

"Well how do you know they're identical?" Vanessa asks. "Can a boy and a girl be identical?"

"No." I shake my head. "And they're identical because they have the same placenta."

"Well aren't you worried that you'll name them legally and they'll grow up with the wrong name?" Vanessa asks. "I mean, if they're identical, then they're going to look the exact same."

"She's right." Madison says. "The only way to tell them apart will be a birth mark. Aren't you worried?"

"Well I wasn't..." I mumble. "But I am now."

"Don't worry." Zane says, brushing my hair out of my face. "We'll figure it out when the time comes."

"Who decides if it's twin? The mother, right?" Colton asks.

"Yeah." I nod.

"But do you even have twins in your history?"

At the mention of twins in my history, I tense up slightly. Nobody notices except for Zane, who puts his hand on my knee.

"I am a twin." I say. Colton frowns.

"What?"

"She's a twinless twin." Finn says. "Our brother died before Bells was born."

Does Finn know the truth? Does Tanner?

At the mention of Reagan being dead, my mother looks out the window of the restaurant.

I want to get to know him. He is my twin, after all. We have the same mother. We shared the womb together.

Something tells me my brothers don't know, and I just feel so angry with my parents.

I hate this selfish thought, but I want the football season to be over so I can go home and confront my family about Reagan. I want to go home and hang out with Reagan.

"When are you due?" Madison asks. "Some time in August, I presume?"

"August nineteenth." I say. "But I'll probably have them before that."

She pauses. "And prenatal vitamins? You're taking those, right?"

"Yes." I nod.

"What brand?" She continues. I know Madison is a nurse and she knows what she's talking about.

"Um..." I think for a moment. "Rainbow light."

"Okay, good, that's a good brand." She smiles.

"Why were you getting blood work done?" James asks suddenly.

Shit.

"She wanted an accurate pregnancy trest." Zane says smoothly.

Madison and James' eyes both narrow at their son, and I think they know he's lying.

"Okay." James says, but I know he's going to question it later.

———

Vote and comment

Also who can't wait for Rose to confront her parents? I'm excited for it haha

~Sam

Chapter Five: Hormones

Chapter Five: Hormones

The entire stadium is on the edge of their seats. I'm gripping my phone so hard, I'm concerned it might break. The score is thirty to thirty, the time paused at twelve seconds. The big screen is on my husband, who has removed his helmet and is in a very heated argument. The stadium is covered in whites and blues and silvers and dark greens and yellows.

I see Zane gesturing wildly with his hands, and one of his teammates, the linebacker, says something, causing Zane to shake his head and continue arguing. He clasps his hands together and read his lips as he says, 'you guys need to trust me'

The coach for the Dallas Cowboys goes marching over to the coach for the Green Bay Packers, asking something, sounding extremely annoyed. The coach for the Packers nods and gestures for the Cowboy coach to go away. Zane seems calmer now. His coach clasps him on the shoulder and talks calmly to him. Zane nods at his words. He shakes hands with his coach and they start to get into formation to kind of wish each other luck. Zane shakes his head and puts up a finger, and then turns around, looking into the crowd. He knows the general vicinity we're sitting in. His eyes lock with mine and he gestures for me to come to the gate. Shit.

I've won the Olympics on national TV, I'll be fine. I stand up and walk down the stair to the stadium. He meets me at the gate, just a bar separating us. The big screen is on us.

"Wish me luck." He smiles nervously.

"I would," I start. "But you don't need it."

His eyes flood with adoration and he leans forward, kissing me. He smells like sweat and grass. The crowd is whistling loudly, and when Zane pulls away, he grinning.

"I love you." He says seriously.

"I love you too." I smile. "You're going to do find. You're Alexander Caulton for fucks sake!"

He laughs and kisses me again, and then he turns around and jogs back to his team. I go back up the stairs and sit down next to Vanessa an Alice again. They get in a circle and put their hands together, and then they all put their helmets on and jog to their positions on the field. I hear the announcers talking about me now, about how I'm an Olympian and blah blah. I see the big screen on me for a moment before it pans back to the field. We wait, and then the whistle is blown and they start going. Zane moves so fast, swiping the ball and running. The time is ticking down quickly, and he only have eight seconds to get all the way across the field. The Cowboys run after him, trying to stop him, and his teammates stay near him in case they have to get the ball again. One of the players is running towards the end zone for the cowboys. They have to make a touchdown.

One of the giant players on the Cowboys runs for Zane and I cringe, gripping Vanessa's hand. He darts right around him and keeps running hard.

When the time hits one second, the crowd is screaming.

And at the last moment, Zane crosses into the Dallas Cowboys end zone, which means he just scored a touchdown. Everyone is on their feet, screaming on top of their lungs.

Since a touchdown is six points, the score is 30 to 36, meaning the Green Bay Packers just won the Super Bowl. My dad and brothers are howling in excitement and the screams in the crowd are deafening. People on the Cowboys team are pissed, but everyone here for the Packers are going crazy. The Packers are screaming and slapping Zane on the back, and I'm so proud of him.

His team starts moving back to their side, and the next thing I know, I'm on my feet, shoving people out of my way. I climb easily over the railing and run straight to my husband, who's walking towards me with a giant s mile.

"Did you see that?!" He exclaims. "That was incredible! Did you see that, Rosie?"

"That was insane!" I exclaim. "You did amazing!"

Alexander

"Jayden and Jordan." I say, rubbing Rose's back.

"No."

"Amber and Abby."

"No."

"Austin and Andy."

"No."

"Megan and Morgan."

"No."

"Laura and Lauren."

She pauses. "Too similar."

"Lucas and Logan-oh wait. Nevermind."

She glares at me

"I'm sorry." I say, glancing around the plane. "How are you feeling?"

"Nauseous." She grumbles. "I think I'm going to throw up again." She starts to get up.

"Want me to come?"

"No." She snaps. "Just stay here Zane."

She stomps off to the bathroom.

I remind myself that she's pregnant and probably feels terrible right now.

After nearly ten minutes she comes back, and I drop a mint in her waiting hand. She pops it in her mouth.

"Please fasten your seatbelts and get to your seats, we will be landing in the next ten minutes."

Rosie puts her seatbelt on and I do too.

"If it's a girl, we should name them Opal and Olivia."

"That's pretty." I smile. "I like that a lot."

"Yeah?" She asks with a soft smile. I nod.

"Okay, Opal and Olivia." She rubs her belly. "If it's a boy, we should name them...Liam and Logan."

"Liam and Logan." I repeat it. "I like that. I like that a lot. The girls should have the same middle name. The same initials." I grin excitedly. "Rosie, I'm really, really excited.

"Me too." She smiles brightly, despite the way she feels right now. "Marley? It's my Nana's first name."

"Opal Marley Caulton, and Olivia Marley Caulton. Okay. Whichever one comes out first should be Olivia."

"I agree." She nods.

"And what about Liam and Logan? Theo?"

"No." She practically growls.

"Okay." I say. I know that she's pissed at her family right now. "Well we can't do Lee. That sounds weird. Liam Lee Caulton and Logan Lee Caulton. E w."

She chuckles, and then she pauses.

"What if..." she swallows, a disgusted look on her face as the turbulence gets worse. She puts her hand on her belly as we start to descend downwards, her head resting against the headrest. "What if their middle names are Alexander, after their Daddy?"

"Liam Alexander Caulton and Logan Alexander Caulton." I pause. "That's a good idea. We need to pick god parents also."

"Do they each get a different one?"

"I think so." I nod.

She hesitates, cringing as the plane touches down on the runway.

"Vanessa and Colton for sure. I think they should have the same one, and then next ones have different ones. What do you think?"

"I agree." I pause. "I want Alice to be included in this, Rose. She's been thinking you're pregnant for months."

"Maybe I can ask her to help me plan the baby shower." She suggests.

"That's a good idea. The babies should call Alice Auntie."

"Yeah. Vanessa can be Aunt Nessy."

"Okay."

The plane rolls to a stop and I can see relief all over her face that the ride is over.

The flight attendant lets us off first and she goes straight for the bathroom. I follow her into the family bathroom and lock the door, holding her hair and she throws up.

"Ugh, Zane, I feel like something is wrong. I want to go to the doctor."

"I don't think something is wrong." I say softly.

"I want to go to the doctor." She insists. "Please?"

Rosabelle

The doctor that will be my doctor until I give birth was much better than the one back in Texas. She reassured me everything was fine and the babies were healthy and happy, and we made an appointment for two weeks. I told Zane I really wanted to go home to rest, so he dropped me off and left in my Chevrolet Suburban to pick up Tank from Aunt Mia's house.

I study the new ultrasound picture with a smile, and then I stick it on the fridge with a magnet.

My eyes wander to the blood test results sitting on my kitchen counter and I frown slightly.

I have so many questions about my twin brother.

What was his life like? Were his parents good to him? Did he do sports? Why did my parents give him up? Do my Nana and Papa know the truth? What about Uncle Shawn and Auntie M. Do Owen and Gabby know? What about Tanner and Finn? What made Reagan reach out to me?

I sigh and walk into the living room, lighting one of the fireplaces.

It's snowing outside because it's only February fifth.

I sit down on the couch and grab my phone.

I decide to text Reagan.

Me: what's your favorite food?

After a minute or so, the message goes to read.

Reagan: pizza. I love pineapple and ham on pizza

Me: fuck that sounds good, I love pineapple and ham on pizza too

I want to see him again. I have so many questions.

Reagan: why do you ask?

Me: I was just wondering. I am having twins btw, I went to the dr today

Reagan: how did your husband take the news?

Me: he took it well. He's excited and I am too

He reads it, and just as he starts typing, the door to the garage opens. I hear the automatic garage door closing, and Tank comes running into the house, straight past me to the doggy door to the back yard. I hear footsteps in the room behind the kitchen, which is like a hall with kitchen counters and a sink and a lot of storage, along with the garage door. Zane comes in with his socks on, his coat removed.

"How are you feeling?" He asks.

"I'm okay." I smile. He sits down with me on the couch and pulls me into his arms. My phone vibrates.

Reagan: does he know about me?

I hesitate.

Me: yeah, I told him

"You should invite him over for dinner." Zane says. "I want to meet him. I know you're curious about him."

I am very curious about my twin. I hesitate.

Me: do you want to come over for dinner tonight?

"What will we have?" I ask Zane.

"Pineapple and ham pizza." He gestures to my phone screen.

Reagan: who will be there

Me: just me and Alexander and our dog

Reagan: I guess so. What time?

It's already four.

Me: now?

I send my current location to him.

Reagan: let me shower first I'll be there in an hour

Me: what do you drink? Alcohol? Water? Milk? Soda?

Reagan: I'll drink anything except for Budweiser. That shit is disgusting

I smile.

Me: i think so too

I hesitate.

"Am I awkward? I feel awkward."

"You're not awkward, Rosie. You just found out you have a twin brother. You know how my Mom told us she was dead?"

"Yeah." I nod.

"She faked her death, and your parents faked Reagan's death."

Realization of that hits me.

"Do you think Tanner and Finn know?" I ask sadly.

"Truthfully? No." He shakes his head. "I think they're in the dark too."

"What about Nana and Papa? And Auntie M and Uncle Shawn?"

"Probably."

"And Gabby and Owen?"

"No, they don't know. Guaranteed."

"I just don't understand why they would lie to me. What if Reagan's life sucked?"

"I don't know, Rosie."

I groan, burying my head in his side.

"Babe, I don't know where to start."

"How about you start with your brothers." He murmurs. "Invite them over."

"I told Reagan it will just be us."

"Then ask Reagan if it's okay if they come too."

"I'm scared." I admit softly.

"Baby girl, I'm right here with you. If it gets to be too much, we can ask them to leave."

I know he's right, and it's better to get this over with.

I grab my phone again.

Me: can I invite my brothers too?

I erase the message before I send it and write again.

Me: can I invite our brothers too?

The message goes to read, and a minute or so later, he starts typing.

Reagan: why?

Me: so we can start somewhere. We're going to have to confront my mom and dad/your birth parents are some point. Might as well start with Tanner and Finn

Reagan: that's their names?

Me: yes. Tanner is thirty three and Finn (finnigan) is thirty one. They're really nice Reagan.

Reagan: okay I guess you can invite them. It's not my house anyways, it's yours.

Me: okay I'll ask

I change the chat to Tanner.

Me: I need you to come over for dinner. Don't ask questions and DON'T tell Mom and Dad

I change the chat to Finn and send the exact same message, and then I wait.

Finn: ok whatever I'll be there in a little while

Tanner: what are we eating?

Me: pizza

Tanner: oh fuck yeah ok I'm omw

Of course Tanner would wait to know what the food is before he says yes. I smile.

"It's going to be just fine, baby girl."

I sigh against his shoulder.

"Can we have sex tonight?" I ask. "Because we haven't had sex in a long time. It won't hurt the twins."

"We can have so much sex that you won't be able to walk afterwards."

Smiling, I tilt my head up to kiss him, and the moment he starts kissing back, I deepen it, grabbing the front of his shirt and pulling him on top of me. I lie down on the couch, and he shifts his stance so he's carefully hovering above me.

"You want to have sex now?" He murmurs against my lips.

"No." I shake my head. "But take off your shirt." I reach for the hem. He draws back and tugs his shirt over his head, grinning down at me.

Dammit, this man is so sexy. Football has made his muscles larger. I reach out to grip his biceps. His abs are well defined. He's so fucking attractive. My eyes wander to his left hand where the wedding ring sits and I grin.

I honestly don't think my life could be better. Everything just keeps getting happier.

I reach up and pull his lips down to mine, kissing him passionately.

————

We snuck upstairs and had a quick round of sex before Tanner got here, and now I sit on the counter watching my two brothers talk about the super bowl last night. My brothers don't know what's about to happen, and I'm not sure how they're going to take the news. My phone vibrates.

Reagan: are you sure this is the right address? This house is huge and I don't see your car outside.

I walk into the foyer and peek through the window.

Me: yeah it's the right house

I pull open the front door and watch at my twin exits a red Chevy Silverado. It's an older version, much like Zane's black Ford F-150 that's from the late 1990s.

He's wearing a pair of black jeans and a red sweater with thin black stripes. His shoes are brown boots. He stuffs his keys and phone into the left pocket of his jeans and walks over to me.

"Tanner and Finn are here." I whisper. "And so is Zane. You call him Alex though. Tanner and Finn don't know who you are and they don't know you're coming over. Do you have that picture of Mom with us as babies?"

He nods.

"Okay." I step aside to let him into the house. "You can take off your shoes and your jacket." I say. He removes them and puts his shoes by the door with Tanner and Finn's shoes. I go into the living room to drape his coat over the back of the couch, and he follows me, his hands still stuffed in his poc kets.

I lead him to the kitchen and my brothers and Zane cut off their conver- sation, and the room falls into an awkward silence.

Zane, of course being the confident social butterfly, breaks the silence.

"Hey, Reagan right?"

"Yeah." Reagan says.

"Names Alexander. You can call me Alex." Zane smiles and shakes his hand, and I notice a hickey on his neck in the same spot I was sucking on forty five minutes ago. Whoops. I snigger, causing everyone to look at me.

"What?" Zane asks.

"You have a hickey." I smile proudly.

"Where?" He asks. I point to the spot on his neck and he just shrugs.

"Whatever."

"I've never heard of a Reagan before." Tanner says suddenly. "Names Tanner. It's nice to meet you." Tanner shakes his hand too. Reagan nods.

"Finn." Finn says, and shakes Reagan's hand.

The kitchen falls into an awkward silence, and Zane moves to my side sensing my unease.

"Guys...I asked you two to come here because I need to tell you something." I tell Finn and Tanner.

"What is it?" Tanner asks.

"Can I have that thing I asked about?" I ask Reagan. He looks at me for a second, almost as if he doesn't know what I'm talking about, and then he digs into it wallet and hands it to me.

"On Thursday night, Reagan messaged me on Instagram telling me he had to talk to me." I tell my brothers seriously. "And he told me he is my brother."

Tanner and Finn's face flood with shock. They both look at Reagan, who looks at the floor at his mismatched socks.

"What?" Finn asks. "No way. There's no way. What's your birthday?"

"April twelfth." Reagan says quietly.

"He was born three minutes before I was." I add. "And look at this picture." I hand it to Tanner. Finn stands next to him to look at it.

"That's Mom!" Tanner exclaims.

"Yeah." I say. "That's Mom. I was still skeptical, so we went to the hospital and got DNA testing done, which is how I found out I was pregnant, but whatever. Reagan is my twin brother, and our parents and probably the rest of the family lied to us about him."

Tanner leans against the counter, rubbing his temples, and Finn narrows his eyes at Reagan.

"You look like Dad." Finn says quietly. "You look more like Dad than Tanner and I do."

"How long have you know about this, Rosabelle?" Tanner asks.

"Since Thursday."

"You've known since Thursday and you didn't tell us?" He asks.

"She has just found out she was pregnant." Zane defends me. "And that night she was taking in the news of having a brother and being pregnant. The next day she was with family all day, and the same with Saturday, and Sunday was Super Bowl, and today was spent on a plane where she was sick, and even though she still doesn't feel good, she's telling you now."

Tanner sighs.

"Right. You're right. Why the fuck would Mom and Dad lie?"

"Reagan, do you have any diseases?" Finn asks.

"No." He shakes his head. "I was born healthy. I was in the foster system for six months and then I got adopted by my parents."

"Are they good parents?" Tanner asks.

"They were at first, but my Mom got cancer when I was ten and she died two years later. My Dad turned to drinking after that...and I've really just been alone since. I don't have adopted grandparents or other relatives, and I was raised an only child. When my Mom died, all I had to hold onto was that picture of my brith Mom and my twin sister."

It hurts me to know that Reagan had a hard time.

Tanner nods at the floor.

"What do we do with this information?" Finn asks finally.

All of us look at our older brother. He sighs slowly.

"I say we confront Mom and Dad." Tanner says.

"What?" Reagan looks panicked. "No. They obviously didn't want me, and-"

"They're not bad people." I say. "Seriously Reagan, they're good people."

"Yeah, they are." Zane says. "And if they start acting like assholes, we can kick them out."

Reagan sighs quietly.

"Alright."

I grab the house phone and dial my Mom's house, putting it on speaker.

It rings three times and then stops.

"Hello?"

"Hey Mom." I say.

"Hey sweetie." She says. "What's up? Is everything okay with the twins?"

"Everything is fine. Do you and Dad want to come over for dinner?"

She pauses.

"What are we having?"

"Pizza."

"Pizza from where?" Dad asks in the background.

"I don't know Dad." I sigh.

"We'll come." Mom says. "What time?"

"Now." I say.

"Bella bear, your mother and I will pick up the pizza on the way over." Dad says. "What kind do you want?"

"Um...cheese, pepperoni, sausage, and...pineapple and ham."

"You want four pizzas?" He asks.

"Actually, can you get two of the pineapple?" I ask.

"Bella," Dad begins.

"She's pregnant Harley." Mama says. "We'll be there with the food in about a half hour. What kind of drinks?"

"We have drinks here." I say.

"Okay." She says. "See you in a bit."

"Okay."

I hang up.

My nerves are getting the best of me and my hormones are messed up.

"I'll be right back." I say, and I walk across the house to the bedroom, lying down on Zane and I's bed.

My relationship with my family was always so strong. My parents loved me and my brothers so much and they were always so honest.

My parents built an entire gym for me in the back yard. My Mom would brush my hair and braid it before school so it would be wavy. They supported me through everything. My brothers and I have a system of stealing the cookie dough with my Dad.

What is Reagan doesn't like football? What if my parents didn't want Reagan for real and they're going to get mad?

Worse, what if we get into a fight and I lose my family?

I find myself crawling under the covers to cry. Tank comes walking in and hops onto the bed with me, resting his head on my belly as if he knows I'm pregnant.

I pull out my phone from my pocket and text Vanessa.

Me: my parents fucking lied to me ness on Thursday my twin reagan texted me and told me that he was my twin and I got blood tests to prove it and he is and that's how I found out I'm pregnant and I told Zane on Saturday or Friday, I think it was Friday, and then I just told tanner and Finn and now my parents are coming over and reagan is fucking here and I'm crying because what if my parents hate me now and i'm scared because what if the twins know I'm crying Nd they're all sad and distressed in there what it me crying hurts them

I send the message, and less than thirty seconds later my phone vibrates.

Vanessa: omw rn

————

Nearly fifteen minutes later, Vanessa was walking into my room with three grocery bags.

"Do you know how fast I drove to get here?" She gasps breathlessly. I'm sitting on the bed sobbing and she seems unfazed.

"Do you want to have a sleepover tonight?" I sniffle.

"Sure." She smiles. "I wasn't sure what you would want to eat while pregnant. I bought takis, sour patch kids, lime chips and salsa, chocolate, and that Talenti ice cream you love. I almost bought beer but I remembered you couldn't have it. How are you feeling? Your brother is alive?"

"He's in my kitchen. I sniffle.

"Rose? Who came in the house?" Zane calls. He walks into the bedroom and raises his eyebrows at the scene in front of him. Oh, hey Vanessa."

"Hey." She says. "I have things under control here."

Zane walks over to me and kisses my forehead, murmurs a soft I love you and then walks out.

An hour and a half later, I'm sitting around my kitchen as my parents talk to my brothers. They have no idea that their long lost son is sitting a few feet from them.

I grip Zane's hand tightly, watching. I've hardly eaten, and Vanessa is watching the scene in front of her. The girl loves drama, but if she's involved in it, she hates it.

"Bella, are you okay?" Dad asks. "You look stressed."

I can't imagine separating my twins. I couldn't do it. I don't get it.

The stress is getting to be too much for me, and I'm just pissed off.

The next words to leave my mouth are completely unstoppable.

"You know babe, if we have boys, we should name one of them Reagan and then give him up for adoption. What do you think?"

The entire kitchen falls silent. Regan visibly tenses. Both of my parents look at me, shock on both of their faces, and then they look at my twin brother. Vanessa looks amused but I can tell she's trying to mask it. I can practically hear her cheering me on in her head.

"Rosabelle," Mom starts slowly.

I pull the picture of her with Reagan and I as infants and slam it down on the table in front of them. Mom looks at the picture and she looks pained, and so does Dad.

"You know, I think I'm going to just go." Reagan says quietly.

"No, you should stay, Reagan." Finn says. "You deserve to be included in this."

"He's right." Tanner says.

Mom and Dad are staring at Reagan and I feel bad for him, so I push myself out of my seat and move to sit next to my twin, crossing my right leg over my left.

"You guys set us up." Mom says slowly.

"You guys lied." I reply calmly. "And we deserve an explanation. Why?"

Mom looks at Dad, who sighs quietly.

"I didn't know I was having twins." Mom admits.

"Bullshit." I say instantly.

"Let your mother talk." Dad says calmly.

"When I got pregnant with Tanner, I was nineteen years old living in a college dorm. My parents were paying for my schooling and I wasn't working. Your father was in the dorm the floor above me. It took one time, and Tanner, I love you so much, but I didn't want a baby. I was a child. I got a job and moved out of the dorm with your father and we struggled for a really long time. Two years later I was still in college raising a two years old and I got pregnant again. Finn, we almost had to give you up because we had to use Groupon to get diapers, but Nana and Papa jumped in and started giving us money, but they were already retired and the government only gives you so much. I was only twenty one. When I was twenty three I found out I was pregnant again. I couldn't afford prenatal care. I was living in a very shitty apartment with a two year old and a four year old that I was struggling to provide for. I was looking for better work and so was Dad. When I found out I was pregnant, Nana told me she would do her best to help, but there was only so much she could do. I couldn't afford prenatal care. I went to a very very shitty doctor when I was six months, and the ultrasound showed one baby, a girl. We got what we could and the apartment was so tiny that we threw out all of Tanner and Finn's baby stuff. We didn't need it. We were having a baby and it was a girl." Mama takes a deep breath, and tears roll down her cheeks. "And then I went into labor, and Reagan, you were breech, which means your feet were first, and they had to put you in position, and when you came out, I was shocked and panicked because you were baby boy, and the nursery at home was pink, but then I had another baby, and it was a girl, and I knew there was absolutely no way in hell I could afford two. Mackenzie and Shawn weren't talking to me and Dad at the time because they thought we were irresponsible. We couldn't afford condoms so he would just pull out." Mom rubs her temples. "Reagan, we loved you very much. We wanted you. We still love you , and we still love you."

Dad is rubbing Mom's back and he looks sad.

"We couldn't afford two." Dad whispers. "Everything at home was already pink. It was nothing against you, Reagan, and speaking truthfully, if you showed up on the ultrasound, it would have been Rosabelle that went up for adoption."

"How did you get the money you have now?" I question. "You clearly had enough to build me an entire gym."

"And the house is huge." Tanner adds.

"We moved from Milwaukee to Bayside and got jobs, good jobs." Mom sniffles.

"Why didn't you go find Reagan?" Finn demands.

"We did." Mom says. "We wrote letters for...for years." She looks at Dad, and then at my twin.

"I didn't get letters." He mutters, picking at a piece of lint on his jeans.

"We sent over a hundred letters to you." Dad says seriously.

"My Dad probably hid them." He grumbles. "Dick."

We fall into silence.

"Can I ask something?" Zane asks quietly.

"Of course." Mom nods.

"Why did you tell everyone that Reagan died?"

"Yeah, what the fuck." I say.

"It was easier for me than to be questioned." Mom says.

"So you just faked your sons death?" Finn asks lowly.

"We didn't fake his death." Mom scoffs.

"Uh, you told us he was dead. You faked his death." Tanner says.

"I'm sorry." Dad says after a pause. "It was easier."

"What if Reagan got the letters?" I demand. "You know his Mom died when he was like, ten? If he got the letters he could have wrote back that his Mom was dead and he wanted you guys to fight for custody. Then what? You'd tell us when he's already on the plane or bus to train to our house that he's alive? I had to find out through fucking blood tests that I have a twin brother!" I slam my hands on the table. I'm pretty sure it's these damn pregnancy hormones that are getting me so mad.

"I'm sorry." Mom says. "There isn't much else to say except we're sorry."

I want them out. I want everyone fucking out.

"Can you guys like...leave?"

"What?" Dad asks.

"Yeah. Get out. Every fucking one of you. Get out."

"What did I do?!" Finn exclaims.

"Nothing." I snap. "But I want to be alone. Mom, Dad, I don't want to fucking talk to you. Tell Aunt Mackenzie, Uncle Shawn, Nana, and Papa that they're fucking dead to me, just like you two are! Now get out! Everyone get the fuck out!"

———

Rose's pregnancy hormones tho :) lmao

Vote and comment!

~Sam

Chapter Six: Emma Scott

A lot happens in this chapter

Chapter Six: Emma Scott

I push myself out of bed for the third time tonight and wander to the bathroom to pee. My belly is swollen now, and it's unmistakable. I'm twenty one weeks and three days, and I have yet to feel the twins move. I know it should be any day now, ad I'm anxious because usually I should feel it between eighteen and twenty weeks.

I have sweat literally dripping down my back. When I finish in the bathroom, I wash my hands, splash cold water on my face, and walk back into the bedroom. Zane is sleeping soundly, and I grumble under my breath about his luck and slip out of the bedroom. I go to the thermostat and study it, blinking repeatedly because I don't have my glasses on or contacts in. It's April and it's like forty degrees outside.

I shut off the heat and walk around the house to open all the windows, letting the freezing air inside.

Thank god.

I get a glass of water and take a sip, and then I walk down the hall to Zane and I's bedroom. I stumble on air and the glass falls from my hand and shatters on the floor, splattering water into the carpet, along with glass. Zane sits up quickly and turns on the side table lamp, his face sexy with sl eep.

"What happened? Are you okay? Why are you awake?"

"I had to pee and then I got water." I mutter. I look at the glass around me. He sighs and pushes himself out of bed. He puts his slides on and picks me up carefully, setting me on the bed.

He comes back with the trash can to the kitchen, paper towels, and the vacuum.

"Why are all of the windows open?" He asks.

I yawn.

"Because it's hot."

"Rosie, it's forty degrees outside."

"And it's three hundred degrees in here."

"But-"

"Zane, I'm sweating." I sigh. "And I've woken up three times tonight already, and it's only two."

"Alright." He gives in.

I watch as he cleans the glass and every time I get up to help him, he just points to the bed.

"You need to sleep." He murmurs.

"I can't get comfortable." I explain, rubbing my heart where the heartburn i
s.

"I know baby girl. I'm going to get that maternity pillow tomorrow." He
says. "The doctor said you can take Benadryl."

"I know."

"You should take some."

"I don't want to."

"Why?"

"What if it knocks Liam and Logan out?"

"I don't think it will." He says.

We found out two weeks ago that we're having boys. Zane is ecstatic and
he said everything is going according to his plan. He's so dramatic.

He finishes cleaning up the glass and then vacuums and then walks over
the spot to make sure there's no glass left, and then he takes everything and
walks out. I hear a door slam somewhere in the house, and a few minutes
later he comes back with more water in a plastic cup with a lid. I take a big
gulp of the ice water and set it down on the side table.

Suddenly, I feel a little wiggle inside of me. I gasp softly and look down.
The feeling goes away and starts again a moment later. It isn't even flutters,
it's actual kicks!

I gesture frantically for Zane to come over here.

"What? What's the matter?"

I lift my shirt and press his hand against my belly. The feeling goes away and starts again a moment later. My eyes well with tears and I look up at my husband.

"Zane, I felt them." I whisper.

"You felt them?" He gasps.

"Yes!" I exclaim.

"Oh my gosh." He smiles. I feel the little wiggle again and I look down at my big belly with a smile, rubbing it gently.

Zane has me lie down, and then he lies down with me and starts talking to them.

———

I sit on the couch with a bowl of cereal on my belly. A random episode of the Kardashians is on, and Zane is out shopping for a pillow to help me sleep. Tank rests his head on my belly, whining softly.

"What?" I ask him through a mouthful of cereal. He looks towards the back door and back at me. "You can go out your door." I say. He sighs and hops off the couch, walking over to his door and hitting it with his paw. It doesn't budge. "So unlock it."

He looks at me and stomps his paw, howling at the ceiling.

"Alright, alright." I grumble. I stand up and walk to his door, turning the key in the lock. He darts outside walks to a spot on the ground, and lies down. "You don't even have to pee, you just wanted to go outside!"

He ignores me.

Huffing, I walk back to the couch and sit down with my cereal, tuning into the TV.

I finish my cereal and drink the milk, and then I put the bowl and spoon in the dishwasher.

I look down at my belly.

"You know if you guys are okay, you should totally kick." I say, tapping my belly. "I know you can hear me. You should kick."

Nothing.

Signing, I walk over to the window to stare at the driveway. When is Zane coming home? I have nothing to do!

I glance at the clock.

10:22AM

Hesitating, I grab my phone and text Madison.

Me: Can I take Alice out of school? I'm bored

Madison: for what

Me: idk for amusement? There's nothing to do and I can't go to the gym because I'm fat

Madison: you are not fat, you're pregnant

Me: please?

It goes to read and three minutes later she messages back.

Madison: I guess so

Letting out a loud cheer, I walk into the bedroom and rip through my clothes.

I put on a pair of jeans that are medium washed and a tan sweater. I put on navy blue vans and grab my purse. I brush my teeth and hair, and then I walk out of the house, groaning when I see that Zane took my car.

I grab the spare key to his truck and get in, grumbling about having to shift.

A half hour later I'm standing in the office of Whitefish Bay middle school, scrolling through my instagram. I told the office I'm getting Alice and now I'm waiting. Alice comes walking into the office with a yellow slip in her hand, looking very confused.

"Belle!" She runs to me and hugs me gently.

"Hey kid." I smile. "Ready to go?"

"Yeah." She smiles. We walk out to Zane's truck. "Where's Zane?"

"Shopping." I say. "What do you want to do? Want to go get our nails done?"

She looks down at her fingers.

"Can I do that with gymnastics?"

"Yeah." I nod. "Just don't get acrylics. One time I got acrylics and my nail fell off. We don't need to go into that. You can get gel."

"Okay." She grins.

———

We got our nails done and then went to get massages. I went to a pregnancy massage but Alice obviously didn't. We went to Babies R Us after and then I took her home.

Vanessa and Colton are coming over tonight and I guess Colton is bringing his new girlfriend. Zane has been out shopping and running to stores and getting maintenance done on my car all day, so he walks into the house with his hands full of groceries.

"Need help?" I ask.

"Not from you." He says, pressing a kiss against my lips before slipping back out the garage door. I start going through the groceries, putting things in their place. He brings in the rest of the groceries, looking at the bags from Babies R Us.

"You went to the baby store and didn't invite me?!" He exclaims. "Rose!"

"Sorry." I cringe. He grumbles about betrayal and starts helping me put groceries away.

"I'm excited to meet Colton's girlfriend. Do you think she's going to be nice? It's been so long since he dated. I hope she treats him right."

"I think she's going to treat him fine." I say truthfully. "Colton isn't stupid. He won't tolerate a bad person."

"That's true. They should be here in about a half hour. What do you want to do for dinner?"

"I don't care." I reply.

"Hug?" He asks, opening his arms. He looks so hopeful. I smile and walk into his arms, wrapping my own around his waist. Hugs are difficult because of my baby bump but he doesn't seem to mine. His fingers rake slowly up and down my back, and then he places a long kiss on my lips. "I love you."

"I love you too." I mumble against his lips. I dart in and kiss him again.

Vanessa came waltzing into my house in pajamas , no makeup, and her hair in a messy bun. She said she didn't. care how she looked today, grumbling about cramps. Now she's laying on my counter with a jar of pickles.

"Are you okay?" I ask her with a laugh.

"No." She snaps. "I feel like shit. What if I'm pregnant?"

"How could you be pregnant?" I ask. "Who are you having sex with?"

She pauses.

"Nobody." She takes a large bite from her pickle.

"You're lying." I accuse.

"Correct."

"So who is it?"

"We haven't decided when to tell you yet."

"It's Finn." I say automatically. Her eyes widen and she sits up.

"What?!"

"It's my brother." I fold my arms across my chest. "But if it's not Finn, it's Reagan."

"It's not Reagan."

"So it's Finn." I say accusingly.

"Well," she starts. I grab my cell phone and dial my middle brother, waiting.

"Hello?"

"Are you in a relationship with Vanessa?"

There's a long pause and then the line clicks. Thirty seconds later, Vanessa's phone starts ringing. I walk over to her and snatch it out of her hand.

"Finnigan Theo Caldwell, the jigs up. Come over. Now." I hang up on him and glare at Vanessa.

"Are you angry?" She asks.

"How long?" I ask.

"What?"

"How long has this been going on?"

"Let's just wait for Finn." She mutters.

I lean against the counter with a sigh.

Fifteen minutes later, my brother comes sauntering into the kitchen, his hands stuffed in his pockets.

"You told her?" He asks Vanessa.

"I didn't tell her anything." Vanessa replies, taking a bite of a pickle.

"Well what do you want to do? Lie?"

"Well considering I'm standing right behind you..." I trail off, glaring at my brother. He turns around with a cringe.

"Hey sis!" He walks towards me like he's going to hug me, but I put my hands out. Zane looks amused.

"Explain." I say. "How long has this been going on?"

Vanessa looks at Finn and they seem to have a silent conversation.

"Since before high school graduation." Vanessa says. "It started while you were in rehab."

"What?!" I bellow. "You two have been dating for twelve years?"

"Thirteen, I think." Vanessa smiles nervously.

They have to be fucking lying.

From the way Finn leans against the counter next to Vanessa though, completely comfortable, and Vanessa seems comfortable too, I know they aren't. Plus, when he came in and asked Vanessa if she had told me, he wasn't rude, he was just asking.

"Who else knows?" I ask finally. They both glance at Zane, causing me to turn towards him.

"I saw them kissing earlier today. I haven't had a chance to tell you yet."

"You saw them kissing?!" I explode. "Where? You told me you were going shopping!"

"I told you I was going shopping and I did, but if you asked me why I was gone almost all of the daylight hours, I would have told you I was at your parents house."

"My parents house?" I snap. "Why?! You lied to me!"

"I didn't lie." He replies. "I told you I was going shopping, and I did, but after I went to your parents house. I was going to tell you anyways. It wasn't planned. If you had asked me while I was there, I would have told you that I was at your parents house."

"Why did you go over there?" I ask.

"I wanted to make sure they were okay." He says calmly.

"That's fucked up." I snap.

"How-"

"When you found out about your Mom, when you went to California, the entire time, if you were having troubles with her, I stayed away because I knew you didn't want me talking to her. I respected you and what you wanted! Even before you found out and she would ask me about things, I didn't tell her! It was your business! You intentionally went behind my back and-"

"It wasn't behind your back, Rosabelle." He sighs, rubbing his face. "You're right. I shouldn't have gone over there without asking you first, but how long are you going to keep up this charade of anger? You're six months pregnant on Sunday. Do you want them to miss everything? You told Alice they can't come to the baby shower? They have been there for you for everything! If Reagan can forgive them, you can too!"

"I never told you when to forgive your Mom! I never told you-"

"That's because it took me like, three days."

"So what?! I didn't tell you how to feel, and-"

"I'm not telling you how to feel. You can forgive them and still be bad. Rose, I'm still mad at my Mom. You're going to reach a point where you will realize you need your parents. Maybe it will be tomorrow, maybe you'll be having contractions when it happens. Maybe it'll be at your baby shower, or maybe you and I will be struggling with two newborns. I don't know. But you will reach that point. I know. I've been there."

"Don't talk to me about this again. I'm not fucking kidding, Alexander. Don't bring it up, and don't talk to them!"

He looks frustrated.

"Are you mad at me?" He asks finally.

"I'm fucking pissed at you. Fuck this. You two kept secrets from me for thirteen years. And Zane? You went behind my back like that...god, fuck t his."

I grab the keys for my car and march into the garage.

"Rose, where are you going?" Zane asks.

"I just need some space."

Alexander

Two hours later I'm sitting on the couch with Colton, his girlfriend Emma, Vanessa, and Finn.

"Well did she go to Tanner's?" I ask Finn.

"I don't know man. Let me ask him."

"Ask Reagan too." Vanessa says.

Just as Finn starts to dial, my phone chimes.

"It's Rose." I say. Finn hangs up and everyone looks at me.

Wifey: I love you and I know you're probably worried. I'm at the gym. I'm just watching. I don't want to fight with you, but I'm hurt you went behind my back like that. Please don't come to the gym. I want some time to think.

I study her words for a while.

Me: okay, I love you too. I'm sorry Rose. Can we please talk when you get home?

When we get into fights, this is about all that happens. Either she's mad at me or I'm mad at her. We don't really yell about it. Whether it's me going to down to the basement to be alone or me going on a drive or to toss a football around with Colton, or her going to the gym or into the study to read a book or watch TV, we take the space we need. After we take space, we sit down to talk about it. I hate the feeling of her being upset with me. It makes my chest feel tight and my body ache.

I think back to about a year ago when Rose backed my truck into our mailbox.

She wrote an apology letter.

"Alex!" Finn exclaims. "Where is my sister?"

"What? She's at the gym. Listen, I'm going to the store. Don't burn my house down."

"Alright."

Rosabelle

I pull into the driveway around nine. I'm dreading them conversation with Zane. I park the car in the garage and rest my head on the steering wheel.

You can do this. Just go in there.

I hate fighting with Zane. It makes my body ache and my chest feel tight.

I push the garage door open and step into the warm house.

When I walk out of the little pantry area and into the kitchen itself, I stop short. There's three giant vases of red roses. Three dozen of them. They're in beautifully intricate vases I've never seen before.

Resting against the middle one is an envelope. I look around the kitchen and into the living room. There's nobody in here.

I grab the envelope and rip it open.

My Dearest Rosabelle (Rosie, Rose, Baby girl),

I remember that time you backed my truck into the mailbox and you felt so bad that you wrote me an apology letter. I decided I would do the same.

I should not have gone behind your back to see your parents. That was entirely wrong. I did it because I hate seeing you upset. I know you don't say it, but you don't need to. I know you. I know when you're tired from one look in your eyes. I know when you're done shopping for the day from the look on your face. I know your favorite TV show. I know your guilty pleasure is the Kardashians. I know you can't wait for Liam and Logan to be born, and I can't either. I know your smile. I have it permanently embedded into my mind, and it's that smile that gets me through hard times. The thought of you makes me feel all warm and gooey inside, and I knew from the moment I walked into your class that you were the one. I know the sparkle in your eyes when you're excited, and sometimes, I know what you're going to say next. I know exactly how far you let that brown hair fall before you reach out and brush it back. Haven't you noticed when I brush your hair back, I do it right before you're about to do it? I can finish your sentences, too. I don't know Rosie, I just know you, and I love you so much, so seeing you hurting about your parents upsets me. You don't know I notice, but I know when you say you're going outside with Tank, you're really going out there to cry. You miss them. You're hurting. You went from talking to your parents every day to not talking to them at all. Your brothers forgave them. I don't see why you can't. I'm not saying that what I did isn't wrong. I know it was. I know you're mad, and you have every right to be. I'm sorry I went behind your back. I'm sorry I didn't ask if you were okay with me going to see your parents. I love you baby girl, I lo ve you very much. I'm sorry.

Love your favorite person in the whole entire world, Alexander Caulton

P.S. I'm in the basement so when you're ready, come down to me. Colton is here with his girlfriend (she's really nice) and Finn and Vanessa are still h ere.

I smile softly. He's so sweet. I know he genuinely is sorry. I fold up the letter and go into the bedroom. I put it in my side table, and then I remove my jeans and shirt and pull one of Zane's shirts over my baby bump. I put on a pair of his basketball shorts and grab my phone from the pocket of my jeans. I walk out of the bedroom and to the basement door, going quietly down the stairs.

"We should call her." Finn says.

"I'm telling you she's fine." Zane says calmly. "She's pregnant, Finn, not broken. Besides-" he cuts off when he sees me coming down the stairs. "Rosie."

Every head turns, and Tank gets up and walks towards me, sniffing me carefully, and then he licks my hand and goes to lie back down on his dog bed. I gesture for Zane to come over to me, and I meet him halfway, stopping in front of him.

He just looks down at me with those sexy eyes and waits.

"You're right, you were wrong." I say carefully. "But I forgive you. I love you. Can we stop fighting now?"

He smiles. "Yes. I love you too."

I wrap my arms around his waist, my belly pressed against his. He hugs me back, placing a tender kiss on top of my head.

I feel a wiggle inside of me, and then a strong feeling. A kick.

"Rosie, why did you just poke me?" Zane pulls away. I grin up at him.

"I didn't. Your son did."

"What?"

I point down to my stomach where it's still jutted out from a limb of one of our twins. It disappears a moment later.

"Come back!" He exclaims, touching my stomach. From the complete other side of my belly, I feel another kick, and then another movement from the other side. "Which one is it?"

"It's both of them." I smile up at him. "They're both kicking."

His smile widens. "That's good, right?"

"That's very good." I smile.

"Does it hurt?"

"No." I laugh. They both squirm around a little bit and then lie still.

"Belle." Finn says. My eyes snap to my brother. "Are you going to talk to Vanessa and I?"

I really don't want to get into that conversation tonight.

"Eventually." I nod.

"Oh yeah." Zane says. "Rose, this is Emma. Emma, this is Rosabelle. You can call her Belle or Bella is whatever else you can come up, just nothing has has to do with Rose's unless it's her full name, because that's my thing."

I look away from my brother to Emma, and my entire body stiffens. She's pale as she looks at me, her face completely blank.

Emma. Oh my gosh. Fuck.

My smile from feeling my sons wiggling around inside of me vanishes, and I can physically feel my face paling.

Everyone looks between the two of us.

Emma. Fucking Emma.

I open my mouth to say something, but I close it.

What the hell am I supposed to say?

I feel myself getting nauseous.

"Uh..." I clear my throat. "I have to pee." I head for the stairs.

"There's a bathroom down here..." Zane trails off. "Do you guys know each other?"

Do we know each other?

I just go upstairs, my heart pounding. I push into my bedroom and into the bathroom, vomiting into the toilet. I flush and brush my teeth, slumping against the counter.

Emma Sofia Scott. Dear god, I accept a very long time ago that I would never see her again.

"Rose?" Zane walks straight into the bathroom. "What's the matter? You know her?"

"I want my brother." I sniffle.

"What?"

"I want Finn."

"But-"

"Please Zane, I need Finn."

"Okay." He says. He walks out, and a minute later he comes back with Finn and Vanessa. Good, I need both of them right now.

"What's wrong?" Finn asks. Zane lingers in the doorway and I gesture for him to come in and close the door.

"Yeah, what the fuck? Who is she? Want me to fight her?" Vanessa asks.

"No." I shake my head. "That's Emma."

"Yeah?" Finn says.

"That's Emma."

"So?" He asks.

"Wait." Vanessa puts her hands up. "Emma? Like Emma Emma? That's Emma? The Emma?"

"Yes!" I hiss. "That's Emma Scott!"

Finn's face floods with recognition.

"Holy shit." He says.

"Who is this girl?" Zane asks. "I'll ask her to leave. Oh god, did she got to high school with you? Is she one of the girls that bullied you?"

"No." I swallow.

"So who is she?" He wonders.

He has every single right in the world to know, and I have absolutely no reason not to tell him. There isn't anybody I trust more than my husband.

"Zane, Emma is-"

And just like that, I'm a sixteen year old again.

———

Theories anyone?Flashback time, get ready *inserts devil emoji*

Prepare to be sad :)

~Sam

Chapter Seven: Emma Scott; Part Two

Chapter Seven: Emma Scott; Part Two

Rosabelle, Sixteen years old, her third day in rehab

My shrink walks with me down the hallway, my arm resting in a sling.

"It's cold in here." I mumble, my eyes locked on the floor. My face is hidden by my hair.

"I know." She says. "Cold air kills bacteria. Did you know that?"

"Bacteria? This is a mental hospital. People with mental illnesses don't have bacteria."

"I know." She says. "How are you today?"

"I miss Vanessa." I whisper.

"I'm sure she misses you too." She smiles softly. "But your roommate is really nice. Her name is Emma."

"What's she in here for?" I ask.

"How about you ask her that?" She stops in front of a white door. "This is your room." She opens the door.

A girl with very wavy dark brown hair, almost black really, and brown eyes sits there, tracing a pattern on her white blanket. She looks up at the sound of the door opening.

What if she's mean? What if she's just like Alyssa Fisher? That girl made a t-shirt of my naked body. What if this girl is just like her?

"Come on in, Rosabelle. Emma is nice, right Emma?"

"I guess." She says dully, looking back at her blanket. She's really thin. I wonder if she has an eating disorder or something.

I step into the room, looking at the empty bed.

I drop my duffel back on it with my right hand.

"Emma, this is your new roommate, Rosabelle. Rosabelle, this is Emma. She's going to be your partner through this. She got here three days ago too. You guys bond, and I'll come get you in a little while for dinner."

Dr. Wilson walks out, the door clicking shut behind her.

Emma and I fall into an awkward silence, and I hide my hair with my face.

What if she thinks I'm ugly too? What if she thinks my ribs are weird too?

My eyes well with tears and I look away.

"You have pretty hair." Emma says softly. My eyes snap to hers. She looks hesitant. Scared, even, and I notice a big bandage wrapped around her t high.

"Thank you." I whisper. "So do you. Do you dye it?"

"No." She sniffles and looks down at her blanket.

"Well it's pretty." I climb into the bed and look down at my own covers.

She likes my hair? She doesn't think my hair is ugly?

"Did you cut your thigh?" I ask. She looks at me.

"What?"

"I asked you if you cut your thigh." I whisper.

She looks wearily at me.

"Yes." She swallows. "But I couldn't get the bleeding to stop, and my Dad panicked and called the cops." She looks down with a frown. "Did you cut your shoulder?"

"Yup. Nicked an artery."

"Did it hurt?"

I hesitate. "I'm used to it." I whisper. "You know if you put cornstarch on a cut it'll stop bleeding?"

She frowns. "Cornstarch?"

"Yeah. They use it on dogs when you cut their nail too short."

"How did you learn that?" She asks.

"The internet."

She chuckles a little.

"You had somebody break your heart, didn't you?"

I look at her, my heartbeat speeding up. "Yes. How did you know?"

"I can see the pain in your eyes." She whispers. "I know that pain."

———

"Just do it." Emma laughs. "Come on. Do the flip!"

"Emma, I haven't done gymnastics in-"

"Whatever! You're going to the Olympics someday!"

"No I'm not." I sigh. I fall onto my bed with a large plop. The happiness is gone. "No I'm not, Emma. Lucas took that away from me."

"Lucas didn't take anything away from you. Everything he has, you gave to him."

I've been locked up in here for two weeks, and it's easy with Emma. She supports me through everything and when I have therapy, I come back and talk to her about it and vice versa. She sits with me while I cry, and I sit with her while she cries. Some nights we share one bed and cry together.

She told me she's in here because she has an eating disorder. She's bulimic, I guess, which means she eats and throws it up. She has severe depression because her little sister died in a car accident when her Dad was driving drunk. Her Dad lived. He's an alcoholic and he beats her Mom, but her Mom saw the cuts and sent Emma away, I guess. Her Dad was drunk when he called the cops. I don't know, but she's had a hard time.

We get each other on a deep level. If I'm sad, she knows why. She can read me like a book.

"When we get out of here Belle, and we're eighteen, me, you, and Vanessa. ..we're going to move. We're going to get an apartment together and stay up late watching movies and eating ice cream and whatever the hell we want. You're going to go back to gymnastics and we're going to talk about our boyfriends and plan your Olympic trip. It's going to happen, I swear on i t."

"I'm never going to have a boyfriend, Emma. I'm never going to get married. I'm never going to have children. I'm never going to the Olympics."

"Yes you are." She insists. "Maybe not now, but one day you will. God, who knows where you'll be ten years from now?"

"Single...alone..."

"Whatever. You're going to find a man one day that's going to shower you in love and romance. He's going to buy you rose's and kiss your cheek and talk to your baby bump. He's going to want you, and not for your body, but the way your eyes light up when you get in the gym. He's going to want you for the way you smile. He's going to want you for you, and one day, you will have sex, and when that day comes, it'll be because you want it, and he's not going to ask for it. He won't ask for it. He will want you to be ready, because he's going to care. He's going to give you massages and cuddle with you by the fireplace, and he's going to be hot as fuck and very handsome, but he won't be out of your league. Rosabelle, one day, you're going to have a man that supports you and sticks by your side through everything. He's going to be in the stands when you're kicking ass in the Olympics. He's going to cuddle by the fire and watch Christmas moves with you, and he's going to put lights on the house with you and smile down at you as you stand in the yard with your pregnant baby, or with your actual babies playing in the snow nearby, and you're going to hold Christmas lights in your hand and he's going to hold the strand and put them on the house. You're going to decorate the three, and he's going to lift your kid up to put on the angel. I don't ever want to hear you say you won't find that life, because you will, and that man is out there somewhere, on this day, he's out doing something. He's alive and breathing, living his life, and making memories he's going to tell you about. Bella, in ten years, you're going to be a completely different person. Right now though, it's okay not to be okay, because one day this is going to be a distant memory."

I have tears gushing down my cheeks as I stare at Emma. The sincerity in her words makes me start to believe them.

"You really think he's out there somewhere?"

"I think he is." She nods. She walks over to my bed and sits behind me, starting to braid my hair.

"You're going to have that life too, you know."

"Maybe." She murmurs. "What do you think your future husbands name is?"

I frown, thinking about it for a while.

"Something classy." I decide. "But still sexy. Like Benjamin...or Sebastian, or...Maxwell. Something that demands attention."

"I agree." She says, "Something long but can be nicknamed. Something sexy and classy. What about Bennett?"

"Maybe Bennett." I nod.

"What do you think he's going to look like?"

"Muscles." I say right away. "Not too much. Just enough to make you horny at the sight of him, but not too much like Dwayne Johnson."

"Hair?"

"Tumblr hair for sure. Dark though, like mine, or yours. Probably closer to yours."

"Eyes?" She asks.

"I don't know? Green? Maybe blue." I smile.

She chuckles.

"One day you're going to tell him about this conversation. What if his name isn't one of the ones we listed?"

"Then I'm sure he's going to tease me about it." I smile.

"You know I'm going to be there right? I can't wait to meet Vanessa."

"I know, I'm so excited." I rub my hands together. "I miss her."

"I know." She squeezes my right shoulder.

————

I walk into my room I share with Emma, excited to deliver the good news. After six long months in here, I get to finally go home.Dr. Wilson is with me, but when I walk in, Emma isn't here.

"Where's Em?" I ask Dr. Wilson, going to my suitcase to back.

"Oh." Dr. Wilson frowns. "Emma left."

"What?" I ask.

"Emma left, Rosabelle. Her parents couldn't afford her treatment anymore."

"What!? No, there's not way. Emma cant leave yet. She's not ready! She'll go back downhill!"

"I know." She says. "But she left."

She left.

"Where did they take her?"

"I think she is moving to England."

"England? No! We're supposed to move in together!"

"I know." She says. "I'm so sorry, Rosabelle."

End Flashback

———

Yeah so I'm gonna end it here. I teared up a little bit :(

Vote and comment

~Sam

Chapter Eight: Emma Scott; Part Three

Chapter Eight: Emma Scott; Part Three

Present Day

"I never saw her again." I whisper at the bathroom floor. "I searched for her for years, Zane. Years. I thought she got worse. I thought she killed herself. I was in therapy for a very long time after rehab because of Emma. I tried to find her to get my Mom to pay for her, and my parents were going to do it, but I couldn't find her." More tears slide down my cheeks. "She's the reason I am who I am today. That girl was with me at my absolute worst. There is nobody who knew me better. Nobody. She could tell what I was feeling before I could. She knew me so well. I thought she was dead!" My voice cracks and I bury my head in my hands. I feel Zane's arms wrap around me. His fingers run through my hair. I cry softly into his t-shirt.

"But she's not dead." Vanessa says calmly. "She's here. You found her. She's in your basement probably freaking the fuck out. Don't you want to know what happened to her? You've been wondering for years."

"What if she's different?" I sniffle, pulling away from my husband. "A lot of time has passed."

"Yes." Finn says, draping his arm around Vanessa's shoulders. "A lot of time has passed, but she seems really nice and Colton really loves her. I don't think she's that different."

"I can't go down there." I whisper. "Colton might not know her past."

"They've been together for six months." Zane says. "I'm sure he knows. How come you never told me about her before?"

"I don't talk about that part of my life." I sniffle. "I never talk about it."

"That's true." He murmurs, rubbing my back in slow circles.

"Do you think she would tell Colton?" Vanessa asks.

"I don't know." I mumble.

Vanessa crosses her arms over her chest.

"Rosabelle, you are a boss ass bitch. Walk your pregnant ass downstairs and ask her if Colton knows." Vanessa says strongly. "Let's go."

I wipe my tears, flick my hair over my shoulder, and march right downstairs.

Emma is talking quietly to Colton and she looks frustrated.

"Does Colton know?" I ask strongly. She stands up.

"Yeah." She says quietly. "He knows, and I filled him in on you. You didn't tell him about me?"

I rub my arm nervously and step further into the basement. Zane puts his hand comfortingly on my shoulder.

"I don't talk about that time in my life." I say quietly.

She toes my carpet with her sneaker and sighs.

"I was right." She says finally.

"What?" I ask. In answer, she nods over to the wall of the basement where five gold Olympic medals are on the wall at the end of a very long line in order of when I got them, starting from when I was four years old.

"You're an Olympian."

"Was." I correct.

"You are an Olympian. Once an Olympian, always an Olympian, although you're not doing much of that nowadays." She looks at my belly and smiles a little.

I move closer to Zane.

"What happened to you, Emma? I thought you died. Dr. Wilson told me your parents couldn't afford your treatment?"

"Yeah, I told her to tell you that." She says quietly.

"Why?" I step closer to her.

"My Mom died." She mutters. "And my Dad, as you know, was a drunk. He pulled me out and forced me to move to England. I relapsed...um, and I almost died...twice, and then I turned eighteen and put myself into therapy. It wasn't enough to fix me completely, but it helped. I struggled until like, three years ago."

"What changed?" I question.

"A news article." She whispers.

"A news article?" I repeat.

"Yeah." She nods. "It said that Rosabelle Caldwell was back to training. I still lived in England, but I kept up with America's information."

"Emma,"

"I had a shitload of money saved up." She clears her throat. "And you did it. You did exactly what I said you would. You're so fucking strong, Belle. I admire you for that. So I put myself into rehab, and a week after I got out was the Olympics, and I found out you were going. I got the last ticket."

"You were there?" I ask.

"I was there." She whispers, nodding. "And I cried like a fucking baby. I was going to come see you afterwards but there were so many people and I wasn't sure if you wanted to see me or not, and I didn't want to ruin your moment so I stayed away. I moved back to Wisconsin. First in Appleton because it was the only place I could find that I could afford, since all my money went to rehab. I moved last September to Milwaukee, and I ran into Colton in the grocery store a month later. I didn't know Colton and Alex were best friends, and I definitely didn't know you were Colton's best friends wife."

"Why didn't you guys come over?" I wonder.

"Because Alex was out of town." Colton shrugs.

"Yeah, I'm not doing that again." Zane says suddenly, causing everyone to look at him.

"What do you mean you're not doing it again?" Finn asks.

"I would have to leave and start practice August fifteenth. Liam and Logan are due August nineteenth."

"They're going to come before that." I say.

"I know." He says.

"So why are you not going back?"

He gives me an incredulous look. Everyone is looking at him like he has two heads. He moves to so I can see him better.

"I'm a father." He says. "Those are my babies. I have responsibilities."

"You don't have to give up your dream-"

"I'm not." He says. "I did what I wanted. I might go back one day, but I'm not going back next season. I'm not going back for a while."

"You can go back, Zane. You don't have to-"

"Baby girl, I don't want to go back." He says. "I want to stay home with you and the kids. I want to be a father a lot more than I want to play football."

All this time I thought I was going to have him for a few weeks and then I was going to have to do be alone.

He's staying with me.

"Maybe if I go back the next year when the boys are one, you guys can come with me." He says. "And I can go until you get pregnant again and then I'll stop, and I'll go back, and we'll keep doing it until the twins are old enough for preschool...if you want."

"We'll see." I say.

"Either way, I'm not being away from my family again. Being far from you is the hardest thing I've ever had to do."

I sigh softly.

"I mean, do you want me to leave?" He asks, and he looks hurt at the thought.

"No, of course not." My phone starts ringing the moment I stop talking. With a sigh, I pull it out of my pocket.

James Caulton

I press answer.

"Hello?"

"Bella? You need to make a baby registry!" Alice whines. "How are people going to know what to buy you if you haven't made a registry!? You need to make two of them! The party is on Saturday, July ninth at two in the afternoon. Now, who's credit card am I using to pay for all of this?"

I open my mouth and close it again, and then I thrust the phone at my husband.

"What?" He asks, taking the phone out of my hand. "Dad?" He listens for a moment. "Credit card?" He repeats. "Well how much is it? What?! Alice! No way, Alice. Where is Dad? Well does he know you took his phone? Well where is Mom? No, Alessandra. Absolutely not. You're going to wait for tomorrow. I don't know!" He shakes his head at me. "I realize that. Just because I'm a football player and I can afford it doesn't mean I want to pay six hundred dollars for-" she cuts him off and he listens for nearly two minutes. "I don't know..." he trails off. "Why can't you go over this with Rose tomorrow? No, Alice. It can wait one night. I'm not kidding." She listens for another moment. "I'm calling Mom." I hear her voice raise slightly and he grins. "Great. See you tomorrow. Love you, bye." He hang s up.

"Who is Alice?" Emma asks.

"My twelve year old sister." Zane says, and then he looks at me. "I told you to let her help plan the baby shower, not do the whole thing."

"She's excited." I shrug. "I don't want to plan a party. I just want people to mail me presents so I can open them alone."

"Are you inviting Mom and Dad?" Finn asks quietly. I look at my brother with a sigh.

"No."

"But-" he starts.

"I said no, Finnigan. Don't fucking ask me about Mom and Dad again."

"Don't fucking cuss at me." He snaps back.

"You're being an asshole." I accuse.

"Well you're being a-"

A sharp pain in my abdomen makes me gasp in pain. My belly is hard as a rock and the pain hurts like a cramp but a million times stronger.

No, this is a contraction.

"Rose? Rosie?" I feel Zane's hands gripping my shoulders. "What's wrong? What's happening?"

"Bella? I'm sorry, I was being a dick. I didn't mean it." Finn says. The feeling won't subside. My breathing is labored as I wait for it to pass, and slowly, i t does.

"Rose." Zane says.

I can't be having contractions! I'm twenty one weeks! The twins have a two percent survival rate!

"Rosabelle." Zane says strongly.

"We need to go to the hospital." I say. "We need to go to the hospital right now, Zane. Right now."

"Was that a contraction?" Vanessa asks slowly.

"Yes! I want to go to the hospital your Mom works at. She's at work, right?!"

"Yes. Yes, let's go right now." He doesn't wait a second to pick me up and carry me upstairs.

———

Vote and comment please!!

~Sam

Chapter Nine: Bedrest

- -

Chapter Nine: Bedrest

I sit in the hospital bed hooked to a ton of machines. There's the frantic beating of my heart and the steady beating of the twins hearts. James is in here with Alice, Tanner and Reagan are here, Emma and Colton, Vanessa and Finn, Zane, and Madison.

I'm so scared. I'm petrified. They can't come out yet. They're safe inside of me!

"Madison, tell me they're going to be able to stop it."

She says nothing.

"What's the worst that can happen?"

She looks at me with sad eyes and I already know the answer.

I turn my head into Zane's shirt and cry.

"Just because that's the worst doesn't mean it's going to happen." She says softly. "They might give you medicine to stop contractions, and then send you home on bed rest."

I look up at Zane and he gives me a small smile.

"Rosie, everything is going to be fine."

I study him, my eyes wandering around the room at the worried eyes.

"Zane." I mumble.

"Yes?"

"I'm scared."

Another contraction starts and I clench Zane's hand. He leans down and kisses the top of my head.

"Me too baby girl, me too."

It lasts for about twenty seconds and then it stops.

Around twenty minutes later, a doctor walks in.

"Where have you been?" I ask coldly.

"Rose." Zane says.

"I was-"

"Probably doing something that could have waited!" I snap. "I'm twenty one weeks pregnant! I can't give birth yet! It's my job as a mother to protect my kids, and it's your job as a doctor to help me! I don't care what you have to do! I'll pay for it! Get me one of those fake uterus' if mine isn't working anymore! I'll pay it! I have a lot of money. I can afford it. Turn them out of the delivery position! Give me pills! Just keep them inside me! I'm not giving birth until they're full term. I refuse."

He looks a little startled, and then he politely kicks out everyone except for Zane and Madison. He checks my cervix.

"You're not dilating or thinning." He says. He removes his gloves and puts on more, and then he lets everyone back in. He pulls my shirt up and does an ultrasound. "And the twins are not in position, see?" He moves the screen and points to my boys, who are still in the same spot they were last w eek.

"Are you dilating?" Emma asks.

"No." I shake my head at her.

"But you're having contractions." The doctor says. "What did you do today?"

"Um...went to the nail salon, went to get a massage...went shopping, went to the gym to watch..."

"Have you been under any stress lately?"

I snort at that.

Have I been stressed? That is a severe understatement.

I found out my twin is alive. I found out my parents lied. I found out my best friend and my brother have been dating for thirteen years, I found out my ex best friend is very much alive and dating my husbands best friend.

"That is an understatement."

"I'm going to give you some antibiotics to stop the contractions. If they don't stop we'll have a problem, but I'm optimistic that they will stop. I'll keep you overnight for observation, and then you're going on bedrest. No shopping, no walking around, no cooking dinner. Drink a lot of water. You can't have sex, and only leave the house for your prenatal appointments."

"Can I fold laundry?" I ask.

"No." He shakes his head. "You can get up to move to the bed and go to the bathroom. Take a bath instead of a shower and avoid stairs."

"My house is three stories!" I exclaim.

"Do you want your children to be healthy?" He replies.

"Yes." I sigh slowly.

"Then you need to do as I say. I don't want to see you back here until you're thirty seven weeks or later."

———

This is a really short chapter. I'm sorry, I'm just going to do a time skip :)~Sam

Chapter Ten: Gasoline

Chapter Ten: Gasoline

I stare at the date on my lock screen, my fingertips running up and down my belly.

I'm thirty seven weeks and two days pregnant. It's go time. I want the babies out so bad. I'm tired of being locked up on the couch. I feel like a four hundred pound bowling ball. The twins are in position and constantly kicking me in the worst places, and it just hurts. I can see their elbow drag across my belly. They're uncomfortable and so am I.

My midwife said they will come when they're ready, but what if I'm ready?

I look at Zane. "Can we go on a walk?"

"No."

"But I'm ready."

"I know."

I think he's just as ready as I am. I'm miserable all the time and sore all the time. We're both sexually deprived since it's been like four months since we've had sex.

Truthfully though, I'm nervous. What happens if Zane seems me open up like that and he gets revolted at the sight of me? What if I never get my body back? All I want to do is take Tank and go on a jog, but I can't.

The nursery's are all set up, the car seats are in my car, and the hospital bags for all four of us are by the garage door.

I can constantly feel my stomach and back tightening with braxton hicks. The twins are squirming slightly in there but they move less because they're so cramped.

"I'm getting up to walk around."

"Rose," Zane begins.

"Let me do it, Zane!" I stand up.

"Okay." He sighs.

I sigh back at him and start walking around the house. He follows closely behind me, and I go to the bathroom and take a shower even though I'm supposed to take a bath, and I put on panties, sweatpants, a sports bra and a t-shirt.

Zane walks with me around the house. It's already ten something at night.

"We should go to bed." Zane says.

"No." I say.

"Baby girl, you need to rest."

"Zane, I have a feeling about tonight, alright? I'm not going to bed."

"What do you mean you have a feeling?"

"I mean I have a feeling." I say, stepping out into the comfortable August air. I walk down the driveway towards the mailbox and turn down the street.

"What kind of feeling?" He jogs to catch up with me.

I pause when I hear a soft popping sound, and then warmth rushes down my legs.

I watch as the gray sweatpants get darker with liquid.

"My water just broke."

"What?" He asks. I grin at him.

"Looks like we're having twins tonight."

"You're kidding." He says.

And that's when the pain starts. It's subtle at first, and then it's much, much stronger. I keel forward and in seconds he has me in his arms, running for the house. He sets me down on the kitchen counter and disappears, coming back with new panties and new sweatpants, along with his wallet and keys, and my purse. He helps me change and carries me out to the garage, pausing when he sees his truck is parked outside of the door, blocking my car in. I moan in pain and lean against the wall.

"We'll take my truck and I'll switch it out later." He says frantically. He carries me to the truck and puts me in the passenger seat.

"Lock the house." I moan.

"Right, right." He sprints back into the house, coming back with four hospital bags that he tosses in the bed of the truck with my purse. He starts the truck and goes flying down the street. I can feel the pain intensifying and I have to bite back screams. Zane is rubbing my shoulder the best he can, pulling away to shift. He pulls onto the interstate and floors it towards Milwaukee.

I cry out again as another contraction hits, and as we're going seventy five down the road, we suddenly start slowing down.

"What are you doing?!" I shout at him. "Oh my god, it hurts!" I sob.

"Rosie." He says. "Please don't panic, okay?"

"What?!" I yell. "What's wrong?"

I grimaces.

"We're out of gas."

"No." I whisper. "No, oh god Zane, n-" another contraction hits and I cry out. He pulls the truck over and we come to a halt. The engine is silent, and all I can hear is my labored breathing and cars zipping past us. "Call somebody!" I yell at him. He pats his pockets and his eyes flood with pure pa nic.

"Rose." He whispers.

"You don't have your phone?!" I yell at him.

"I'm sorry!" He gasps. "Oh god, oh my god!"

"No! You don't get to freak out right now! I'm in labor!"

"Okay, okay." He swallows, shutting his eyes momentarily. He reaches up to turn on the light and then cusses, slamming his hands down on the steering wheel. The contractions are so close together that they're practically consistent, and they hurt so bad that my hands are shaking. I feel like I have to push.

"Zane, they're coming right now." I whimper.

"What?!" His eyes widen.

"They're coming right now. I need you to help me get my pants off."

He doesn't move.

"Alexander!" I shout at him. He jumps slightly and springs into action, helping me get off my seatbelt first, followed by my sweatpants and my panties.

"Don't pull them by the head, okay? You're going to have to take them out. Grab them by the armpits, but support their head, because they can't hold it up by themselves."

"I know." He swallows. His eyes are full of fear. A really strong contraction hits, stronger than any other ones. I rest my head against the window of his truck and cry out in pain.

"Okay." He says. "How do you know when to push?"

"Now." I swallow. "I can feel it. Right now."

"You're going to push right now?" He whispers.

"Yes." I gulp. My chest is rising and falling rapidly. The contraction passes and a few seconds later it starts up again, and I take a deep breath. "Zane, I can't do with without you." I whimper.

"I'm here. I'm right here. I'm ready." He leans forward to place a kiss on my forehead. "We've got this."

"Okay." I say, the pain making me ready to cry.

He pushes my legs open. "Okay." He says again.

"Should I lay on something?" I whimper.

"I'm not making you move right now. The seats are leather Rosie, and they're the least of my concerns right now."

"Okay." I gulp.

"Alright. Ready?"

"No." I whisper, and then I start pushing. I push as hard as I can, screaming in pain. I pause for a second to catch my breath, and then I start again, crying from the pain, crying from the insanity of this situation. Tears stream down my cheeks.

"Okay, okay Rosie, stop." Zane says. I stop pushing, gasping strongly. I feel him reach down and through the darkness of his truck, I see a tiny little baby in his hands.

"Is he alive?" I rasp.

A moment later, a loud cry fills the truck.

"Logan." He says. "Welcome to the world little man."

"He's still attached to me, Zane. Can I push out Liam? Check the clock!"

"I don't know." He says. "Dammit Rosie, I don't know." He has one hand on Logan's head and the other one on his butt. I reach out for him, but he shakes his head. His truck is luckily one of those really old one that displays the clock 24/7.

10:44PM.

"Logan was born at 10:44PM." He says. "I can see Liam's head, baby girl. What do I do with Logan?"

"I don't know." I gasp. "I don't know Zane." Tears gush down my cheeks as I look at my son still in his arms.

He scoots back a little bit and lies baby Logan on the seat, who is still screaming.

"Okay, okay." He says. His hands are covered in goo and blood, along with his jeans, and so is Logan.

"Make sure he doesn't fall, Zane. Don't let him fall." I say. I'm in so much pain and I just want to push Liam out.

"Okay." He says. He won't fall, I promise."

Sniffling, I nod.

"Okay sweetheart, push."

I push again.

"Stop!" He says. I stop pushing, and he reaches inside of me and I feel him pull little Liam out of me. "He's not crying, Rose, and he's not breathing!"

"Okay, give him to me." I order.

He hands Liam to me and I cradle him in his arms.

"Go in the diaper bag. It's in the bed, alright. There's a blue thing in there. It's. Blue sucky thing. Get it!"

He gets out of the truck quickly and I sit up slightly to put my hand on Logan's chest. Liam remains silent and I start to panic, planting a tearful kiss on his forehead. I look at the clock. 10:48PM. Zane comes back with the blue bobby thing, and I practically snatch it out of his hand and stick it up Liam's nose, sucking out all the goo on both sides. I do the same thing to his mouth and cradle him, holding my breath.

A few seconds later, a loud cry fills the car, and tears gush down my face. Zane shuts the door to the truck and picks up Logan.

"Okay." I shut my eyes. "Zane, we need help. We need to get to the hospital."

"Where is your phone?"

I look at him. "On the couch."

He looks like he's about to cry or something.

"Give me Logan." I say. "Give me him."

He gently sets him in my arms and I sit up, resting both of them on the seat in front of me with help from him. I pinch both umbilical cords and look up at my husband. With a shaky voice, I say; "Now run for help."

"What?!" He gasps.

"Run for help, Zane. We need help. You need to get help. Go get help. Anything. Anyone. Grab a phone and dial 911, call your Mom, call my Mom, call anyone. We need help!"

"Okay." He looks scared. "Are you going to be okay? What if something goes wrong?"

"Nothing is going to go wrong. Go get help, Zane!"

He darts forward and kisses me, and then he kisses both babies and gets out of the truck. He takes one last look at me through the window and starts running down the interstate.

"Everything is okay, alright babies? Everything is going to be fine." I feel tears burn my eyes, my voice trembling with fear as I whisper, "Daddy will come back."

———

VOTE AND COMMENT OK I AM FREAKING OUT RN YOU GUYS~SAM

Chapter Eleven: Hospital

Chapter Eleven: Hospital

I've been sitting here for what feels like forever. It's 11:30 already according to the time on Zane's clock. The twins are laying close together, sleeping peacefully. I wrapped my sweatpants around them in case they went to the bathroom. I want to get them to the hospital to get them clothed and cleaned. I'm so scared. When is Zane going to come back? It's been almost an hour!

I notice strange marks on Liam's arm, and I lick my finger and use my saliva to wipe off the goo. He has marks all down his right arm. A birthmark. It goes from his shoulder to his wrist. Logan stirs slightly, sticking his thumb in his mouth.

Liam makes a sucking sound, suckling with his mouth, and then he moves a little bit, and I put my hand on his belly because he's closest to the edge.

I hear a noise in the back of the truck and twist around. Zane. Oh thank the lord.

He does something in the back and tosses a red tank for gas in the trunk, and then he opens the passenger door, his eyes wide.

"Are they okay? Are you okay?"

"Yes, we're fine."

"How are you feeling?" He asks, looking at me and then our sons.

"I'm sore." I admit. "And very tired."

"Well I ran four miles to a gas station and got a red tank and put some gas in the truck, and then I ran back." He smiles softly at me. "Are you sure you're okay?"

"Yes Zane, I just want to get to the hospital so the twins can get checked out."

He nods in agreement and pushes the clutch in, starting the truck.

The engine roars to life, and both twins stay sound asleep. He helps me lift them safely into my arms, and then he puts his truck in first gear and starts driving, carefully pulling back onto the interstate.

The radio is shut off and he's driving so carefully that people are going around him.

"Why are you going so slow?" I ask.

"Because you don't have your seatbelt on and the twins aren't in car seats." He says calmly.

I say nothing else, I just look down at our boys, one head in the crook of each of my arms. I have the cords awkwardly pinched between my fingers.

"Are you okay?" He asks me.

"I'm tired." I reply.

"We're going to go to my Mom's work, because she's on call tonight."

"Okay." I say.

The drive to his Mom's hospital is much shorter than the one in Milwaukee, and fifteen minutes later we're pulling into the ER.

Zane gives me a soft kiss on the cheek and gets out of the truck. He comes back less than a minute later with Madison and a wheelchair. He's talking quickly to her, and I shift slightly so he can open the door.

"Oh god." Madison says.

"Meet your grandsons." I laugh anxiously.

"You pushed them out right there? Without an epidural?"

"Yes." I nod.

"Give me one minute, okay?" She says. I nod. She peeks over my shoulder at the twins and smiles, and then she rushes back into the hospital.

Around a minute later she comes back with a tray. She had gloves on this time and a doctor is with her. She puts the clamp on the umbilical cords and cuts them, freeing my babies from me.

"Liam is the one with the birthmark." I inform her. "He came out second, at 10:48, and Logan came out at 10:44."

"Okay." She says. She reaches out and plucks the nearest baby, Logan, from my arms, passing him off to Zane. She takes Liam and hands him carefully to the doctor. Zane hands Logan to his Mom and reaches out. They cover me with a towel and Zane carefully helps me out of the truck. I grip his hands tightly. I feel a little gush below me and look down to see blood running down my legs.

"It's okay." Madison says. "It's the afterbirth. It's just the placenta and the cord."

They wrap me in a bigger towel and then set me to sit down in the wheel-chair.

"Are our twins healthy?" I ask the doctor.

"They seem very healthy." He nods. "We'll do a full examination."

"What about Liam's birthmark? That's safe, right? Don't tell me you have to do a biopsy!"

"We'll find out when we get upstairs." He says. "I'm sure it's fine."

The doctor holds Liam and Madison holds Logan.

We go up to the fifth floor and everything is a whirlwind, the twins being taken to get washed and people having us sign birth certificates and papers, and me getting examined and the twins getting examined. A nurse even examines the placenta to make sure everything was okay with it. They make us quiet down for tests on the twins hearing and things like that, and then Zane slips out and comes back with all of the hospital bags, and I put a diaper on Liam and Zane puts one on Logan, and Liam gets a long sleeve nay blue onesie and Logan gets a white long sleeve onesie. There's two hospital cribs in the room, one with the name Logan Caulton and the other with the name Liam Caulton

Logan is fifteen and a half inches and weights five pounds and four ounces. Liam is fifteen inches and weights five pounds and one ounce. They're both under the weight they would be normally but just by a tiny bit. The doctor said they're extremely healthy, and they finished all the tests. It's well past three in the morning now. Zane is sitting in the chair next to me holding Liam and I'm holding Logan.

Now that there's no threat and everything is calm and they're all clean, I get to examine their features.

They have my nose for sure, and my eye shape, but Zane's blue-green eyes. They both have heads full of brown hair, but there's no curl to it so it seems like they have my hair. Their lips are Zane's, and they seem to have my head shape and chubby cheeks. They're so perfect, so adorable. I'm so happy. Madison left about an hour ago to go make phone calls for us, and she came back in after ten minutes or so. She said Vanessa and Finn are on their way, along with Tanner. Colton is coming with Emma. Mrs. Bennett promised she would be by in the morning, and the same with Mr. Turner. James is coming with Alice, and Reagan said he's coming also. Even Owen and Gabby, who are in town for the twins' birth, are on their way.

Right now though, it's just my husband and I, and it's so peaceful. Logan moves slightly in his sleep and makes a small noise. I glance up at Zane with a big smile.

"We did it." I whisper. "We made it."

"Yes we did, baby girl. We're such amazing parents. You pushed out two babies with no drugs and I pulled them out of you and ran eight miles for gas. I'd say we did amazing."

"I agree." I smile.

He looks at me seriously then. "Thank you, Rose." He murmurs.

"For what?" I smile.

"For gifting me with our boys. For giving me a chance. I'm so happy, Rose. You make me so happy, and life just keeps getting better and better. I love you, baby girl."

"I love you too." I whisper. "Thank you for not giving up on me. Thank you for being exceptional, and thank you for gifting me with our boys. It was a team effort though, and you did all the work."

"What do you mean I did all the work?" He chuckles.

"On Thanksgiving." I laugh softly. "I wasn't on top, you were."

He laughs softly, nodding to himself.

"I did do that, but you did the real work. You created two little angels inside of you. You went through nine months of discomfort, nausea, sitting around, which I know drove you crazy...you know most doctors refuse to deliver twins vaginally without an epidural?"

"I know." I say. "It hurt, but it's okay. It was so worth it."

I look down at our little angels with a soft smile.

I hear a very soft knock on the door and then it's pushed open.

Alice peeks her head in, her brown eyes wide with excitement, but her face is full of sleep. Her hair is a mess and she's in a gray tank top with a pair of pajama pants that have pink polka dots on them.

"Can I come in?" She whispers. I nod, and I'm just excited for everyone to see how precious our boys are. She steps inside the room and James follows her. He looks really excited too, and his hair is messy also.

They both inch closer, and Alice puts her hands over her mouth as she peeks at the twins.

"They're so cute!" She whispers. "Who's who?"

"That one is Liam." I nod down to the baby Zane is holding. "And this one is Logan."

James peeks at them too, looking extremely excited.

"Wow." He says, his hand resting on Alice's shoulder. "Look at them. Those are Caulton boys for sure."

"Right?" Zane says. "They're going to grow up with all the ladies."

The door is pushed open again and Vanessa walks in with Finn. Their eyes are wide too, and I notice how each of them walk like they're going to step too loudly on the floor and disturb them.

"Why didn't you call when you went into labor?" Vanessa whispers.

"That's a very long story." I murmur.

Tanner comes walking in next, with Reagan right behind him.

It's funny to watch everyone step in. Madison walks in with her scrubs on, looking proudly down at her grandsons. Owen and Gabby come in next, and they all crowd around Zane and I, looking so afraid to make such a loud noise. Lastly, Colton and Emma come in, looking excited but afraid to make too much noise.

"You guys make cute kids." Emma murmurs.

I feel so happy, but there's an emptiness inside of me. It takes a moment for me to place it. I look at my husband.

"Zane?" I murmur. He lifts his eyes from Liam's face.

"Yes?"

"Can you call my Mom? Please tell her to get Dad and come."

I can see him fighting a smile. He carefully lies Liam down in front of me, places a kiss on my temple, and slips out of the hospital room.with Zane gone, everyone inches closer.

"So, um, you're not like, holding that one, right?" Alice asks, pointing to Liam. "Which one is he again?"

"Liam." I smile.

"Right. Liam. So you're not gonna hold him, right? So I can like, totally do that, right?"

I chuckle softly.

"Go wash your hands and wait for Zane to come back."

She grins widely and rushes to the sink to wash her hands.

She comes back, and right when she reaches my side, Zane walks back in the room.

"They're on their way." He says. Alice looks at me hopefully.

"Alice is going to hold Liam." I inform him.

"Okay." He yawns."Any of you want to take pictures for me? I don't have my phone."

The twins were passed around to each person before coming back to me hungry, and Madison made everyone except for Zane turn around, and she helped melancholic each baby on each nipple, with Logan on my left and Liam on my right. It feels weird to have them suck on me like that, but it's o kay.

They all turn back around once I'm covered, and when the sucking changes and I'm sure they're both using me as a pacifier, I make everyone turn again and hand Logan to Zane to burp him.

I cover myself back up and tell everyone they can turn around and put little Liam's head on my shoulder, patting his back firmly enough to get him to burp. He lifts his head a little bit and I wish I could see him, but I can see Logan, and his eyes are the exact same shade as his Daddy's. I smile. I'm just so happy.

I hear a little burping sound omit from Liam.

"When do I stop?" I ask Madison.

"When you think you need to." She shrugs.

I pause my hand for a moment on Liam's back, but I feel like I should do it more, so I keep doing it, and a few moments later he burps again, and then I move him to settle into my arms, pulling off the burp cloth from my shoulder to wipe his little mouth.

Zane does the same thing with Logan, and then I just look at both of their faces.

"Gosh, they're so cute." I murmur, looking down at him. "They're like carbon copies of one another."

"How do you know that Liam isn't actually Logan?" Emma wonders.

"Because Liam has a birthmark on his arm." I yawn. I'm exhausted.

I hear a soft knock on my door, and then it opens and my Mom peeks her head in. She looks really nervous to be here. I smile warmly at her, and I feel really really happy that she's here. She smiles a little and pushes the door open some more and steps fully into the room. Dad steps in behind her. They both creep up next to the hospital bed to look at them, and Mom has tears in her eyes.

"They're beautiful." She sniffles.

"This is Liam." I say, putting my hand on the chest of the newborn in the navy blue onesie. "And this is Logan." I put my other hand on Logan's chest. "Liam has a birthmark on his right arm."

"They have your nose." Dad whispers softly, a smile on his face. "And your eye shape."

"Zane's eyes though." I smile. "And his lips."

"Gosh, they're like exact copies." Mom murmurs. "Can I?" She gestures to them.

"You have to wash your hands." I say.

"Me too?" Dad looks so hopeful. I laugh a little and nod. They practically fight each other to get to the sink first, and Mom wins and walks over to me

"Take your pick." I say. She grabs Logan first, cradling him in her arms. Dad takes Liam, and Mom has tears in her eyes. She looks at me.

"Did you have a c-section?" She wonders.

"Oh god, my birthing story could make it in the papers." I admit.

"What do you mean?" Alice asks.

"Around...tenish, I felt my stomach tight. I thought it was braxton hicks, but it was labor. I went walking around the house with Zane and my water broke, so we threw everything in the truck because it was blocking in my car and headed for the hospital." I sigh, rubbing my forehead. "About ten miles or so from the house, on the freaking interstate, Zane's truck ran out o f gas."

"You're kidding." James says.

"I'm not." I say. "And I don't really know how to explain it, but when you're in labor...you just know when you have to push. So I did, and I gave birth to both of them on the side of the interstate. Our phones are home. Logan was breathing but Liam wasn't, and I had to suction his mouth with the little sucker thing." I swallow. "And then I sat in the car for an hour with them still attached to me pinching the cords."

"While I ran to the gas station for gas. When I say ran, I mean I was running. I ran eight miles there and back." Zane sighs.

"You pushed them out without an epidural?" Mom asks, shocked.

"Yeah." I sigh. "It was so painful." I cringe at the thought and put my hand on my empty belly.

"Who's older?" Vanessa asks.

"Logan." I yawn. "By four minutes. He came out at 10:44 and Liam came out at 10:48."

"That's insane. Nobody stopped to see why their was a random truck pulled over?" Dad asks. I shake my head and sigh softly. I'm really tired.

"Rose, you need to go to sleep." Zane says. "You have had a very long night. The twins are sleeping. They just ate. You go to sleep."

"You all should leave." Madison says. "Everyone go home and get some rest. You should come back in the morning."

They all look like they don't want to leave.

"Rose needs to sleep." Zane says firmly. "And the twins need to sleep, and I need to sleep. You guys come back around ten tomorrow morning."

"If you think you're sleeping until ten, you have another thing coming." James chuckles.

"Whatever, ten, alright?"

"You can all come back." I say, glancing at my parents so they get the message.

They all kind of grumble and my parents reluctantly give me back the twins, and then they each kiss the top of my head.

A couple minutes later, everyone is out of the room. Zane rolls the cribs over to me and helps me lie the twins in their own bed. We cover them with the blanket.

"Can I go pee?" I ask Zane.

"Yeah." He yawns. He helps me to the bathroom and stays with me until I'm done. When we go back to the room, and helps me change out of the stupid hospital gown and into a fresh pair of sweatpants and one of his t-shirts. He stays with me until I'm in bed, and then he tucks me in. "I love you baby girl."

"I love you too handsome." I murmur. He kisses my lips and shuts off the light. I hear him kissing our sons' heads and then he gets on the couch. I hear him wiggling around for a few minutes and then silence.

It's weird sleeping in such a small bed, so I pull up the sides in case I almost roll off and shift slightly

"Rose?" Zane breaks the silence. "Are you still awake?"

I hum in response.

"I love you." He says. "And I just want you to know that sleeping in a bed without you is my least favorite thing ever."

"I love you too, and me too. I can't wait to lose the bump."

"I can't wait to have sex." He mutters so quietly that I don't know if he meant for me to hear him. "I know baby." He says louder.

"Zane?" I murmur.

"What?"

"I can't wait to have sex too."

He's quiet for a moment. "You heard that?"

"I did." I giggle. "Tomorrow you're going to have to go home and exchange cars...and clean your seats."

"I will."

"And stay there for an hour to let Tank play, and make sure to feed him, okay? And unlock the doggy door."

"I will." He murmurs. I hear him shuffling and then footsteps, and then he leans in close and places a kiss against my cheek. "I love you." He whispers.

"I love you too."

He kisses my cheek again and then gets back on the couch, shuffling around uncomfortably for a while.

Once I'm almost asleep, I hear him whispering again.

"What?" I mumble.

"Are you up?" He asks. I sigh slowly.

"Yes."

"Do you think the twins will play football?"

"Maybe." I murmur. "Who knows what they'll do."

We fall into silence and I start to nod off again.

"Rose?" He whispers. I sigh slowly.

"What, Zane?"

"We make really cute babies."

"I know." I say into my pillow. I'm drooling and I don't even care.

"Rose?" I sigh softly. This man. I love him. "I love you."

"I love you too." I murmur.

He's quiet for a while, and I slowly reach the state where you're sleeping but you can hear, and I think I hear him whisper something but I fall asleep fully before he can.

Chapter Twelve: Conversation

Chapter Twelve: Conversation

I hear shouting down the hall of the hospital and I frown, looking around the room. The babies are sleeping happily in their cribs, little pacifiers hanging out of their mouths. What is all that screaming about?

The hospital room is empty aside from me and the babies, but I want to know what's going on.

Since the doctor said it's okay for me to be up and walking around, I push the covers off of me and walk over to the door. I push it open slightly to peek down the hall, but Zane is on the other side of the door reaching for the handle.

"Did you feed Tank?" I ask him.

"Yes." He says. "I got everything you asked for, I fed him, and I took him on a walk."

I smile. "Okay."

He gently slips into the hospital room and sets down the bag I asked for. I shut the door again.

"Why are they screaming?" I ask him.

He scoffs at that question.

"That screaming it a mother who gave birth around the same time last night as you."

"Well what happened?" I ask. He pauses, as if deciding if he wants to tell me. "Zane?"

"A nurse dropped her baby."

My hand slaps over my mouth.

"What?" I whisper.

"A nurse dropped her baby." He repeats. "And I guess she took the baby to the nursery...when she was told not to, and she gave the baby a bottle when she's breast feeding."

"Is the baby okay?!" I whisper frantically. "Who the hell drops a newborn?" I look at our sons with a frown. They're so little. They weigh less than a gallon of milk, and they're only three inches longer than a ruler.

"The baby is...I don't know Rosie, but the Mom is out there screaming at the nurse."

"Well she's not coming in here." I say firmly. "I don't want her in here."

"I don't either. If she drops either one of our boys, I'm suing."

"I agree." I climb back into the bed. "Who does she think she is anyways? I can't believe-"

We both jump when we hear a loud cry coming from the crib. I walk over to them and peek inside, and see Logan crying loudly, his little arms flailing around.

"Don't cry Logan, it's okay." I murmur, reaching in to pick him up.

"Is he hungry?" Zane asks.

"No, he just ate twenty minutes ago." I say. I remove his swaddle and check his diaper, which is empty.

With a shrug, I grab the burp cloth and put it on my shoulder, and I lift him up and begin burping him. He whines a little bit more and then falls silent, and a moment later he spits up.

Zane has a giant grin on his face.

"What?" I smile.

"Nothing, I'm just so happy."

Smiling, I step forward to give him a kiss. He accepts gratefully.

When Logan has calmed down completely, I wrap him back up in a swaddle and put him in his crib. He's awake still, but Liam slept right through his brothers antics.

I hear a gentle knock on the door and my Mom peeks her head in.

"I know you guys said ten, but we were excited..." she trails off. I glance at the clock. It's nine thirty.

"You can come in." I say. She slips into the room and Dad follows behind her.

"What's with all the commotion?" Dad asks.

"Some nurse dropped a newborn." I explain. "And gave the baby a bottle when it's being breastfed, and took the baby to the nursery after being told no."

"That's horrible. Is the baby okay?" Mom asks.

"I don't know." I reply.

"How are you feeling Bella Bear?" Dad asks.

"I'm fine. I want to go home so I can work out."

Dad looks at Mom with a triumphant grin.

"You owe me twenty bucks."

Mom sighs. "Not yet, Harley."

"Wait, twenty bucks for what?" I ask.

"We made a bet that you would be back to working out as soon as you could. Ivy said you wouldn't but I told her you would."

"Oh, yeah she's going to be back as soon as she can." Zane says. "It's all she talks about."

"Do you know how hard it is to sleep with a stomach that looks like an enormous tumor?" I ask. "I'm used to being able to run twenty miles in two hours. I've been stuck on the couch for like three and a half months."

"You were on bedrest?" Mom asks suddenly. "Why?"

"I went into labor at twenty one weeks." I explain. "Well not really, I was having contractions but they weren't in position and I didn't dilate."

"That's weird." Mom says. "Do they know what caused it?"

"Uh...yeah, it was stress." I rub my arm awkwardly.

They both get kind of quiet and I feel my anxiety level rise. Zane puts his arm around me and pulls me against his side. It's almost as if he's doing it to remind me he's here.

"Belle, are we going to talk?" Mom asks softly.

I put my arm around Zane and move closer to him.

"Can we talk another day when we're settled at home? We're getting discharged tonight or tomorrow...I don't want to have this conversation in the hospital."

"That's fine." Dad says.

————

I stand in Logan's nursery, watching him sleep peacefully. The blue pacifier rests in his mouth and he suckles softly. He looks so peaceful. My parents are coming over tonight, along with my brothers, my cousins, my grandparents, and Uncle Shawn and Auntie M. As I study my one week old son, what happened to my parents makes me sad.

I can't imagine how hard that must have been. They didn't know they were having two because they couldn't afford prenatal care. Then two came out and they could hardly afford me.

That must have been miserable. They gave up Reagan because they genuinely knew that they couldn't afford him, they knew they couldn't give him the life he deserved.

I don't get them telling us that Reagan wasn't alive, but honestly...I don't care. I want my sons to be born into a family that doesn't have problems, so that's what I'm going to give them. I'm going to forgive and move on. If my brothers, especially Reagan, can forgive, then I can too.

I hear footsteps coming up the stairs.

"Rose?" Zane murmurs. "They're here, baby girl."

I turn to him fully.

"I'm nervous." I admit, and he smiles a little.

"It's okay." He says. "I'll be right with you the whole time, unless one of the boys wakes up. Everything is going to be just fine."

"Okay." I mumble. He walks downstairs first and I follow behind him, clutching the baby monitor in my hand.

When I walk into the living room and see my family, my anxiety level rises even more.

"Hey." Mom says. "How are you doing?"

"Fine." I say quietly. I don't want to have this conversation.

I feel myself relax a little when I see Vanessa is here, but only for a moment.

"Where are the babies?" My Nana asks.

"Sleeping." I say, rubbing my arm anxiously. I look to Zane for help, but I know he wants me to nag I ate my way through this. I know this is my problem, it's my job. He's here for support. "Listen, let's just cut right out the chase." I say."I don't want to sit here and have a long heartfelt conversation. I'm getting a few hours of sleep a night. Long story short, you guys were really fucked up for not telling us the truth."

"Bella," Dad starts.

"However," I cut him off, putting my hands up. "I understand why you did it. Not the lying part, but giving up Reagan." Mom takes a deep breath and they all wait. "You knew you couldn't give him the right life. You couldn't afford him. Yes, boys can wear girls clothes too, but you had given up Finn and Tanner's clothes, and you would have to buy double diapers, double clothes. I would yell at you for not wearing a condom, but since you could hardly afford to feed you family, I doubt you could afford condoms. Finding a job probably wasn't that easy. You were fresh out of college and you didn't have enough time, and with twins...it's hard to work. I get it. You guys were...it was fucked up to lie to us."

"Yes, it was." Mom says. "But Belle-"

"But I don't want to sit here and be pissed off anymore. I'm done being mad. I don't want Logan and Liam to be born into a family that has problems. You guys love us, you understand what you did was wrong. There's nothing else to it. There isn't anything else you can do but apologize, and you have so many times I have lost count. Can we please just put it behind us and go back to normal?"

"Yes." Mom says. "We can do that."

"Does this mean me and Vanessa are of the hook?" Finn asks hopefully.

"Wait, she knows?" Owen asks.

"Yes." Finn mutters, shooting Vanessa a look.

"What?" She asks. "You know it's a relief."

"Everyone knew?!" I exclaim.

"Yeah." Dad says. "I've known since before it even happened."

"What the hell?" I ask with a small smile.

"I just don't get why I wasn't told." Zane whines. "I mean, what the hell Finn? You, Tanner, Colton and I...we hang out all the time. Why didn't you tell me?"

"Because you're a snitch." Finn says.

"I am not!"

"Bullshit." Tanner says. "You tell Belle everything. She's your best friend, I respect it, obviously, but we can't tell you things that Belle can't know. You're going to tell her."

Zane hesitates.

"Of course I'm going to tell her. She's my Rosie."

"Exactly."

"Did Colton know?" I ask suddenly.

At the look on my best friends face, I know he did.

"How long ago did he find out?!"

"Uh, you remember way back when, when we were hanging out at that stupid party on the beach?" Vanessa asks.

"When I told off Alyssa?" I ask.

"Yeah." She says. "Well uh, Colton saw us making out."

Gross.

"Why didn't you guys tell me?" I demand.

"Truth?" Vanessa asks. I nod. "Because Bella, you were depressed for years after rehab."

"No I wasn't." I frown.

"Yes you were." She says. "The girl you were before Lucas...she was gone. Lucas took her away from you, and I know you thought you were happy because you weren't cutting anymore, but I sat back and watched you be uptight. You would flinch at the sight of anybody remotely attractive. It somebody would hit on you, you would freeze up. You were uptight and you went home, and the sparkle was gone, and you were just...there. I don't know how to explain it. You were there, but there was always a part of you that was gone. You were depressed."

She's right. I know she's right.

"And I knew why. Everyone in this room knows why. I wasn't certain at first." She hesitates. "Do you know what made me realize things were about to change?"

"What?" I ask quietly.

"We were in the cafeteria the day Alex started." She says carefully. "And he told you that he heard through the grapevine that you two were married." She smiles. "And you told him you were sure he spread the rumor, and you got your food and went to leave and Alex grabbed your arm and you were pissed. Everyone watching could tell you were pissed, and when you get pissed...I mean you sometimes intimidate me when you're pissed." Everyone in the room chuckles and nods in agreement with her. "But Alex looked amused. He was amused and he just asked how he ruined your reputation, and you told him he could stay away from you." She laughs.

"And I said oh, I can. You give me permission?" Zane says in the exact same sassy humorous tone. I laugh brightly.

"And I told you that you didn't need permission, because I'm me and I can tell you to stay away."

"Right." He murmurs. "And I told you that I wasn't going to stay away from you because I'm an adult and that means I get to make my own decisions." He grins. "My favorite part is coming up. This is what made me almost fall in love with you."

"I told you that you knew nothing about decisions." I smile.

"And I asked you what made you say that." He grins so widely I'm worried his face might break in half or something.

"I told you that since you were standing in front of me, it was safe to assume your parents weren't conscious enough to make the decision to use a condom. That if they couldn't make decisions, it could be hereditary, and if there was a very small chance that it wasn't, then I asked you, and I quote, 'please make the decision to stay away from me.'"

"And truthfully, I was floored at this point. I've been sassy since I was old enough to talk. I learned it from my mother."

"You got your confidence from your father." I comment.

"Yes I did." He puffs out his chest. "And I told you I was hurt you thought so little of me, and I said 'but I suppose I'm lucky here, you know, since my genetic inability to make decisions has made it so I can't decide to stay away from you.'"

Vanessa is smiling.

"And then you walked off, and Belle, you were so fucking mad your whole face was red and you walked off from the other door. Things changed that day, because finally there was somebody who could throw your bullshit back in your face. There was somebody willing to tolerate your mood swings."

I smile a little, looking down at the baby monitor.

"Yeah but you got really annoyed of me really quick, especially when I asked you if you were waiting for me to suck your dick." I snort. Zane smiles a little bit.

"I knew right then." He says.

"What?" I ask.

"I knew you being so rude to me had nothing to do with me right from that moment. Truthfully, I thought you were a lost cause...and then you told me to meet you in a deserted pitch black park and asked me to be patient...and then I told you about Alice..."

"That was when I realized you were nothing like Lucas." I whisper, looking down at my hands. He frowns.

"Why?"

I look him right in the eyes.

"Because you were going to kiss me and you stopped."

"You stopped?" Gabby asks. "Why?"

Zane's eyes search mine for a long time before he replies.

"Her hands were shaking." He says. "And I knew she didn't want me to kiss her, so I told her I wouldn't do anything she wasn't ready to do...and I drove her home." He shrugs slightly.

"Lucas never would have done that."

"That's because Lucas is a dick." He says. "I hate that guy with a burning passion. I hate him as much as I hate Alicia, and that's saying something."

"Listen Belle, the point is, when Alex came around, that sparkle came back and you were trying so hard not to let it consume you. When you said you were going to see Lucas, I knew right then and there was it was a good thing. Why do you think I didn't follow you?" She smiles a little. "I knew it was a good thing, because it was closure, and you had needed it for years. What Lucas did to you followed you around for years. I knew it was a good thing when Alice talked about gymnastics with you."

"That's when we decided we wanted you guys to get married." Dad chuckles. "Because my little girl was back. Alex, there isn't a day that goes by where I'm not grateful for you. What Lucas took from Belle, you took it back and gave it to her. I don't know, but the reason she is where she is today is because of you."

He's right. I know he's right.

Dammit, I'm so happy. I turn to Zane with a smile.

"I love you." I say seriously.

"I love you too." He smiles. He places a soft kiss on my lips.

———

You guys should like, so like, totally like, comment

K thanks lmao

~Sam

Also this has like 12 chapters or something and it already has over a thousand reads, I'm really happy about that you guys, I love all of you readers

Chapter Thirteen: Insecure

Chapter Thirteen: Insecure

I sniffle, staring at my phone screen. Tears stream down my face and I fight back a sob. I pull my pillow over my head and just cry. My phone rests on my giant belly. I hear the bedroom door close as Zane comes back for finishing up getting Liam to bed.

"Rose?" He asks. "Are you crying? What's wrong?" I feel the bed sink down next to me and I don't move. I feel him grab my phone to look at the screen. "Who is that girl?"

I sit up so fast that he jumps.

"That's me!" I snap at him. "Look! Look at my b-body, Zane!" My voice is reaching hysteria. "I h-had abs! My arms were p-perfect with m-muscles and s-so were my legs! I was b-beautiful! Now you're all a-attractive still and I'm j-just your fat w-wife!"

He looks startled.

"Do you e-even love me a-anymore?!" I hiccup. "Because you said 'oh who is that' as if she's more attractive than me! You didn't even recognize me! You hardly kiss me anymore! You don't touch me! Y-you're digested! Admit it Zane, you're disgusted!"

"Baby girl, don't talk like that." He says. "Don't ever say that."

"We can't even cuddle the same anymore." I whimper. "We can't even hug." I bury my head in my hands and sob, my entire body wracking as sobs rip through me. "We haven't had sex in months." I sniffle.

I feel his hands rubbing up and down my bare back.

"Rosie, baby girl, sweetheart." He peppers kisses all over my face. "Don't cry, darling. Don't cry." He kisses my neck and my shoulder. I turn my head to press against his shoulder. He sits cross-legged in front of me and I bury my head in his shoulder and clench the fabric of his basketball shorts in my hands he sits there with me, running his fingers through my hair and up and down my back.

Once I've calmed, he speaks.

"Why do you think that? Where did this come from?"

I stare down at my hands.

"I feel disgusting, Zane. I'm an athlete and I haven't been able to go out and do anything. I feel enormous, and...and you saw me exposed on the seat of your truck and you watched me push out two fucking babies. That's...it's gross, Zane. It was gross. You saw me so disgusting like that. You must be disgusted of me. How fucking gross. Before that, you only saw me if I was about to have sex with you. You...you saw me when I was pretty."

"Hey." He says firmly. He pulls back and takes my face in his hands. My eyes glisten to tears as he forces me to look him in the eye. "Trust me Rosie,

I have lost no affection for you. If anything, I'm more attracted to you now than I was before. You pushed our two babies. I can't even begin to imagine how much that hurt, but you did it, and you sat there and you knew what to do. You kept them alive. You created two lives inside of you. You grew them, suffered with feeling crappy and ill and being forced in the house, you hated it. We haven't had sex because we can't have sex. I asked who it was because you were crying. If somebody that everyone finds really attractive walked in here naked versus you, I would pick you. You are beautiful. You are so insanely beautiful. You'll get that body back. You will get that life back, but you only pushed out two babies a week ago. You still have the baby bump. That's okay. You're so strong baby, and you're beautiful. You're so fucking beautiful. Don't ever think you're anything but beautiful. You are beautiful. I love you Rosie, I love you so much."

"You promise?" I sniffle. "You promise you still think I'm beautiful?"

"I promise." He whispers. "Even if you were four thousand pounds, I would still have sex with you."

"I hope I never gain more weight."

"If you do, I'll love you just the same, if not more." He says seriously.

I sniffle again.

"I'm not happy in my skin, Zane. I'm happy in my life but I can hardly look in the mirror. I know people think I'm being ridiculous, but I'm used to being one hundred and fifty to two hundred pounds of pure muscle. I'm so grateful we have Liam and Logan, and I'm so thankful for the life we have, but just because I'm happy we have kids doesn't mean I'm happy with what it did to my body. I want to hire a personal trainer that works specifically with people that have just had a baby. I want to, Zane, and then I want to go back to gymnastics. I won't go back to the Olympics because it's too much for us, but I want to go back to where I was before. I'll do this every single time we have another child. I want to hire a personal trainer. Please?"

He studies me for a long time.

"You don't need one." He says stubbornly.

"But-"

"But if that's really what you want..." he sighs. "I'll make some phone calls."

I sigh and look down.

"I feel stupid for crying."

"You're breastfeeding." He says. "And that does all kinds of shit to your hormones. It's okay. Every time you cry even if you're not breastfeeding and we're old and wrinkly, I'll be here to wipe your tears."

"Do you promise?" I sniffle.

"I promise." He draws an X over his heart.

"Zane don't tell anybody about the trainer, okay? Can it please stay between you and I?"

"Of course." He says. "Your secret is safe with me."

———

When I wake up the next morning, I'm startled because I didn't wake up from the sound of one of my babies crying. Zane's side of the bed is cold. The light on the baby monitor is off, which means it's not on.

I panic slightly and rush out of the bedroom and upstairs. Both nursery's are empty.

What the hell? The twins are way too young to go out in public.

I rush back downstairs to the living room, and I relax when I see Madison holding one baby and Alice holding another one.

"Where is Zane?" I ask.

"He went to the store." Madison says. "And he asked us to come over and watch them so you could get some sleep. We have absolutely no idea who is who though, but this one is hungry." Madison holds up the newborn.

I walk over to the twin and look down at him.

"Well?" Alice asks. "Who is it?"

I shrug.

"Good question." I say. I adjust my son and maneuver him under my shirt. He latches on and sucks happily. A moment later the other one starts up.

"Uh oh." Alice says.

I shift the baby I have and hold my other arm out for the other one.

"You're going to carry them both at once?" She asks. "Won't you drop them?"

"No." I chuckle.

She carefully places my other son in my arms, and I walk off to my bedroom.

"Do you need help?" Madison calls.

"No, but you guys can follow me so you're not alone."

I hear them walking behind me.

I place both infants in the middle of the bed, and the one I was feeding starts screaming when he's forced to stop. I grab the big maternity pillow off of the bench at the end of the bed and sit down, wrapping it around me. They both look away as I reach for one baby and attach him to my left one, his body going down the pillow. It's hard to do with my giant baby bump, but I manage. When his mouth latches onto my nipple, his cries fall silent. I do the same with the other one, pulling my shirt over their heads since my shirt is very loose and light.

"You guys can turn around now." I say.

They both turn around and carefully sit down on the bed. Zane and I have a California king.

"What happened to that nurse that dropped the baby?" I ask Madison.

"She got fired." She says. "Thank god."

I nod in agreement with her. I hear a door slam somewhere in the house.

"Mom?!" Zane calls. She doesn't respond in fear of startling the twins. I hear his footsteps and then he walks quietly into the room. "I told you guys there was breast milk in the fridge!"

"Sweetheart, my body is basically on a timer." I remind him. "Every time they need to eat, I'm awake. I can feel it. I woke up."

"You can feel it?" He repeats.

"Yes."

"Where?"

"In my boobs."

He hesitates.

"Okay. It's Logan with the birthmark, right?" He asks.

"No sweetheart, it's Liam."

"Are you sure?" He asks. "I think it's Logan."

I hesitate, and the image of them laying covered in goo on the seat of his truck flashes in my head.

"No Zane, it's Liam."

He hesitates.

"Liam was on the right in the car. He was on the right, and he was the one with the birth mark."

"Okay, I trust you." He kisses my lips, and I notice how he does it longer than he usually would. He pulls away then. "I love you Rosie, you're beautiful."

"I love you too handsome." I smile. He kisses me again.

"Well we have to get going." Madison says. "School starts on Monday and we haven't done any shopping."

It's Saturday, August 12th. The twins were born Friday, August 4th.

"Okay." I say. "Thank you for coming over."

"You're welcome. Any time."

Zane walks out with them.

A few minutes later he comes back.

"Male trainer or female trainer?" He asks. "If you still want one?"

"Female."

"I found one already then." He says.

"You did?!" I ask. "What's her background?"

"She's a fitness instructor and she's willing to work with you five days a week." He informs me. "Her name is Amber, she's thirty, she has three kids, and with the routine she was doing, she lost all the weight within four months."

"But did she have twins though?"

"She had triplets."

I can physically feel my face light up.

"Can you tell her to come over please?""Rose, I'm worried you might get pushed too hard and wind up in the hospital." He says. "You are beautiful just the way you are."

"Zane, I am an Olympic athlete." I remind him patiently. "Just like you are an athlete. I can tell when my body has been pushed too far."

He seems hesitant, but he gives in anyways.

Chapter Fourteen: Squirt

- -

Chapter Fourteen: Squirt

I stare at the twins in the living room, watching the twins sleep happily.

At two months old, they're both very healthy, at nine pounds now. They're out of preemie clothes and into newborn, and I'm so happy. The baby bump went down naturally and I meet with Amber five times a week to workout. I can run about five miles in total right now. I have a some loose skin on my belly, which is okay. I'm working on it, and Amber taught me to accept it. I'm a Mama. I'm a very proud Mama. It's okay.

The twins had their doctors appointments and they're doing great. I'm such a proud Mama. They're perfectly t their two months milestones. They can do tummy time for five minutes each, although Logan doesn't like it very much. They smile when we talk to them and if they hear a loud sound, they cry, which is normal for their age. They open their hands instead of keeping them in tight fists, they see Zane and I and they know we're Mommy and Daddy, and they can lift their little chests off the floor on tummy time, and they can hold their heads up for a little while but it's shaky. They're so flipping cute.

I hear the garage door open and shut and my husband comes walking into the kitchen. I see him setting groceries on the counter, and then he walks into the living room.

"I was thinking Rose..." he starts, giving me a kiss. "We should take the twins to a pumpkin patch and get them matching outfits and take a really cute picture. It's not just us anymore. We have a family of our own, that we created together. I want to take really bomb pictures so I can brag about my sexy wife and attractive children to my six hundred and fifty thousand followers."

"Okay, I'll post them to my 1.2 million." I smile sweetly at him. He scowls.

"You know what Rose? The only reason you have so many followers is because you're famous worldwide."

"That's what being number one does to you." I shrug innocently.

"Brat." He says, his lips twitching with a smile. He lunges at me and I stifle a squeal as he tackles me onto the couch, climbing on top of me. He tickles my side and I struggle not to scream in laughter. He lowers himself down on top of me with a giant smile on his face. "You're cute, Rosabelle Caulton. You're very cute."

"You're very handsome, Alexander Caulton." I smile up at him.

Truth is, he is very handsome. He has blue-green eyes and a vanilla and mint scent. He smells just like home to me. There's a slight stubble on his face and he looks tired, but he's so perfect. A lock of dark hair falls out of place. He reaches up and brushes it back, and I just lie there and admire him.

He didn't do his hair today, he just combed through it. I reach up and slowly run my fingers through it, and then I guide my hand down to rest on his right cheek. My eyes lock with his, searching them for a long time.

The two month appointment was this morning, and while Zane left the room to go to the restroom, I asked the doctor if we could have sex and he said yes.

It's been nearly six months, and he doesn't know.

"You know?" I murmur.

"What?" He asks. His voice is rough and I've been married to him for three years this month. I can tell when he's hard by one look at his face.

"When you left the room at the doctors, I asked if you and I could return to having sex, and he said we could."

His eyes widen and he swallows. I can physically hear it.

"And um...do you like, want to? You know, right now?"

I glance over at the twins and he does too.

"They're buckled in." I say, running my fingers through his hair. "They're safe in there, and they look so cozy...I would hate to, you know, be loud in here and wake them up. We could-"

"I'll get the monitor." He says, and he springs off of me. I sit up, and I'm actually nervous, so I do the only humanly female thing. I grab my phone, open the chat with Vanessa and send her a quick text.

Me: WE'RE GONNA HAVE SEX I'M VERY EXCITED I'LL LET YOU KNOW HOW IT GOES

I put my phone on silent and set it on the couch.

Zane comes rushing back in to plug in the baby monitor. He takes the other end and grabs my hand, pulling me to our bedroom.

He turns up the volume and turns to me.

"You buckled them in, right?"

"Yes."

"And you're sure you're ready?"

"Yes."

"And um, well, I don't know what to do with your boobs Rosie, because there's milk in there now, and-"

"Let's just wing it." I say. I pull his shirt off in one fluid motion and start backing him up to the bed, removing my sweatpants. He takes off his jeans and socks and walks towards me in a black pair of briefs. I stile a groan at the sight of him hard. He grabs my hips and I feel my body fall against the mattress.

"How long have they been in the swing?" He asks suddenly.

"Like, ten minutes, Zane."

"Okay." He says. "Rosie, are you sure-"

"Yes." I say. I reach out and pull his mouth onto mine. What starts as soft and gentle turns to frantic, and he pulls my shirt off. I didn't bother with a bra because I've been around the house all day. He grabs my hips and moves me into the middle of the bed. He starts kissing down my jaw, tugging at my panties. He hasn't seen me so openly since I had the twins right in front of him, and I'm terrified he might not like what he sees.

Still, he slides my panties off of me easily, and then he pauses at the sight of me
.

He hates me. He hates me. He hates me. He hates-

"Rosie, you are so radiant, baby girl." He says. "I love you so much."

He doesn't hate me.

"I love you so much too." I whisper emotionally. I reach out for him, and his lips press against mine again. It feels like there's a sudden change in the atmosphere, as if it's our first time again. I reach for his boxers and pull them off, my eyes never once leaving his. He lowers his body closer to mine, placing soft kisses on my face. He pauses at my lips.

"I love you so much, so very much, and I'm feeling very emotional and very in love right now and I'm not sure why." He places a gently kiss on my lips. "But I love you. I love you so much."

I draw back a little bit to see his face, smiling softly at him.

"So am I, baby. I love you too. I love you so much too."

And then he's kissing me again, but suddenly he draws back from me.

"What?" I ask. "What's wrong?"

He looks down at his chest, and I see a very liquidity white substance running down his very defined abdomen.

"What is that?" I prop myself up with my elbows. Frowning, he touches it with his finger and raises it to his lips. "Zane? What is it? Don't you know not to eat foreign things?"

He smacks his lips a little bit and then starts roaring in laughter. He's hunched on his back legs upright looking down at me and roaring in laughter.

"What?" I ask, laughing a little.

"It's m-milk!" He gasps. "You shot me, Rosie!"

"Milk?" I repeat, and then I remember I'm a mother and it's milk. My milk.

I shot him with breast milk.

I start laughing with him, and we both lie there, completely naked, laughing our asses off.

If this isn't a happy marriage, I don't know what is.

———

"What?" Vanessa asks."You what?"

I snicker at the memory and whisper into my phone. "I shot him with milk."

"With breast milk?" She asks. "During sex?"

"Well he wasn't in yet, but yeah, basically."

She starts laughing, and I laugh softly, folding the onesie in my hand and setting on the pile of Liam's clothes.

"Belle, listen...when you're pregnant and you feel the baby move for the first time...what does it feel like?"

I'm quiet.

"Why?" I ask slowly.

"Wondering." She says.

"Flutters." I say. "You were having symptoms like, five months ago." I remind her,

"Yes. I took a test with Finn and it was negative. I haven't gotten nausea or anything. I can't believe you squirted on Alex." I hear howling in the background. "Shut up, Finn!" Vanessa yells jokingly. "She shot breast milk, not actual squirting!"

"Have you gotten a period?"

"Yeah, like...three months ago, I think, but I looked it up and three months ago to now is only what's it-"

"Twelve weeks." I say.

"Right." She says. "And you don't feel the baby move until like, eighteen weeks."

"That's at the earliest usually. Some people feel it super early but that's ally if they were pregnant before." I pause. "But I didn't feel the twins until twenty one weeks. The period you had three months ago, how heavy was i t?"

"It was light." She says.

Logan's sucking changes on my nipple and I can tell he's using me as a pacifier. I have the pillow around my body so he can eat without me having to hold him. It's just Zane and I home so v completely exposed. Liam is sleeping on Zane's chest and Zane is watching Family Guy. He offered to help but I declined, and now he's just relaxing. He let me sleep in until ten this morning because I'm sure he gave the boys bottles of my milk when they woke up.

"How light is light?"

"Light enough that I didn't need a tampon or a pad or even a panty liner, even though I used one anyways because I got this new underwear, and-"

"You're pregnant."

She scoffs.

"No I'm not."

"Yes you are." I argue.

"Who is that?" Zane asks.

"Nobody." I reply.

"Women." He grumbles. I laugh softly.

"Who are you talking to?" Vanessa asks. "Is that Alex? Shit Belle, you can't fucking tell him."

"I'm telling you you're pregnant. You haven't had a period in months."

"So?"

"Your boobs are bigger." I remind her.

"Well...well..."

"You had spotting." I continue.

"Yeah, but-"

Liam starts crying on Zane's chest.

"Hold on." I tell Vanessa.

"He's hungry, Rose." Zane says.

"Come take Logan and burp him please, baby." I say.

He walks over to me and hands me Liam, taking Logan. I put Liam on the other side and guide his mouth to my nipple. He latches on and suckles quietly.

"What do I do?" Vanessa whispers into the phone.

"Go get a test." I say. "Or tell my brother."

"We're not even married." She mutters. "I'm fucking petrified dude, what if I'm a shit mother?"

"You won't be. You're great with the twins. You'll be fine."

"I already have a test." She says.

"Where's Finn?" I ask.

"I knew it was Vanessa." Zane says. "Maybe we have telepathic skills, you and I."

"Finn is watching fucking family guy." She grumbles.

"So is Zane."

I turn my attention to Liam, who just spit up. I wipe off my breast and his mouth. He starts screaming suddenly, and I pick him up so his stomach is across my left arm, his head resting by my elbow. My left hand grips his diaper gently and I start patting his back.

After crying loudly for another minute, he throws up on my leg.

I sigh softly and start rubbing his back. He spits up a little more, and I move him onto the pillow, and then I wipe my leg off with a burp cloth. His blue-green eyes peer up at me, wide open.

Feeling better?" I ask him. He coos loudly and then grins.

I can hear Vanessa peeing on the other line.

"Are you doing it right now?" I ask her.

"Uh, yeah." She says. "Dude, if I'm pregnant, that means you're biologically related to my kid."

Liam coos again, begging for attention. I smile down at him.

"Hi baby." I grin. "Hi. Hi little one. Hi Liam."" I tickle his neck and he coos again, his little hands waving around in the air. "Gosh Zane, we have really good genes."

"I know we do. Look at these godsend children, eh?"

I smile at his comment.

"Uh, Rose?" Zane asks.

"That's not Liam."

"Yes it is."

I slide up to right sleeve to his onesie and see no birthmark.

"Oh, just kidding, hi Logan."

"I'm relieved to know it's not only me." Zane laughs softly.

He whines softly, so I put him back on my nipple and go back to folding clothes.

"I'm tired Rose." Zane says.

"You can go to bed." I say.

"But it's early." He says.

"So? You had dinner. The kitchen is clean. I can handle the boys."

"I'm just going to wait for a little while longer." He says. He settles down on the couch again, this time with Liam, the actual Liam, and not Logan.

I keep folding clothes at Logan nurses.

"Rosabelle?" Vanessa asks into the phone.

"Yeah?"

"I'm pregnant."

"What?" I ask.

"I'm pregnant." She repeats. "Fuck."

"I'm gonna be an auntie?" I ask.

"Yeah. Holy shit, I'm fucking scared. What does it feel like when the baby moves?"

"Flutters." I say. "You'll know when they kid though."

"Don't say they." She says. "I can't have twins. Fuck dude, who decides twins? The Dad or the Mom? Because you're a twin, which means that Finn has that in his bloodline, right?"

"Right, but I think it's the Mom." I say, moving my phone to the other side.

"I'm going to look it up. Be quiet so Finn doesn't know we're still on the phone."

"Alright." I reply.

I hear her typing on her phone and I glance down at Logan. He's so cute. I'm so happy. I glance at Zane then and see he's sleeping with Liam on his chest.

I mute the microphone.

"Zane." I say. He doesn't move. "Zane." I repeat. Nothing. "Alexander!" I exclaim.

"What?" He whines, moving his hand to Liam's head.

"You need to put the baby somewhere." I tell him.

"No, he's warm and we're cuddling."

"Sweetheart, if you roll over while he's on top of you, he could fall off the couch."

He groans softly.

"Is Logan still eating?" He asks.

I look down at the infant on the pillow in front of me. I can tell he's sleeping.

"No, he's using me as a pacifier."

"I want him." He says.

"Zane." I sigh.

"I won't drop them. I promise."

I maneuver my arm under Logan's small body and pull the pillow out from underneath me. I walk over to Zane and hand him the infant. He moves to his side and rests the twins next to each other. He pulls the blanket over himself and both babies, and he puts his arm across them so they're safe. I lean down and kiss all three boys, and then I pull my shirt over my chest and line the floor below them in pillows.

I sit down to start folding laundry again.

"Belle?" Vanessa asks. I unmute the microphone.

"Yeah?"

"Twins usually come from the Mom but some people say they don't believe it because they have no twins in their bloodline but the husband is a twin or whatever and they end up having twins. Dammit, I can't have twins dude, I'm freaking out."

"I don't think you're having twins. If you're five months, you would be showing. I had a slight bump at three and I was pure muscle."

"So I'm not five months?"

"Not if you're having twins."

"I'm going to tell Finn." She says.

"Good luck. If he does anything stupid I'll drive over there and beat his butt."

She chuckles. "Alright."

We hang up and I set my phone down.

When the laundry is finished, I put all the folded piles in the basket and head upstairs, putting random outside in each room.

I promised myself when I was pregnant that I would try to remember who's outfit was who's, but they look the exact same anyways so I stopped caring. They wear whatever I put them in.

I go back downstairs and see all three of them fast asleep.

Zane is laying with his left arm outstretched across the couch, his head resting on his bicep. Both twins have their arms up by their heads. They're both suckling, their lips pursed, and Zane's mouth is slightly parted, his chest rising and falling steadily, and his right arm is throw across the babies, holding them against the couch.

They look so peaceful and it's the cutest thing I've ever seen.

I grab my phone and take a picture of them, and I send it to Madison and my Mom, and then I set it as the lock screen.

I take the remote and change the channel to the Kardashian's, sitting down on the other couch.

————

Yay Vanessa is pregnant! <3Girl or boy? Twins?Comment your vote!~Sam

Chapter Fifteen: Talk

- -

Chapter Fifteen: Talk

I'm anxiously cradling Liam to my chest, my forehead creased in concern as he cries.

"He's probably teething." Mom says calmly, walking over to me.

Logan is lying in Vanessa's arms chewing on his hand.

"I don't know what to do. The doctor said I can give him Tylenol but he's only two months old."

"Just don't give him a lot." Madison says. "You have baby Tylenol, right?"

"Yes." I point to the diaper bag. She digs through it and gives me the right dosage, and I give Logan the medicine.

He takes. It and then screams louder. I pick him up and bounce him lightly.

We're into the middle of the month of October now and the twins are teething. Logan is screaming and Liam is biting things and he screams too and normally when he's not screaming, Logan is, and when Logan stops

Liam will start. Zane and I are hardly sleeping but I feel like I'm about to have an emotional breakdown.

Zane is in the basement with the guys and I'm upstairs with the girls, and Zane went down there when they were sleeping and I'm trying my best to leave him alone because he's working so hard to make sure I get enough sleep and he picks up the slack when I'm with my trainer.

He deserves to have some time.

Liam starts crying then, and I don't know what to do, I don't know what to do.

"I'm going to get Alexander." Madison says.

I open my mouth to argue but she's already walking off.

I pick Liam up from Vanessa and he keeps crying and I hold two ten week old babies as they scream their heads off.

My eyes fill with tears and I feel like I'm about to explode.

"What can I do?" Alice asks.

"I don't know." I say. "Oh my gosh, please stop crying. Please." I beg.

"Rose? Why didn't you come get me?" Zane asks. I turn around, and he looks worried. "You're not a single mother." He reminds me.

"You always pick up the slack." I say. "And you were downstairs."

He takes both of them from my arms.

"You need to go calm down." He says.

"No, I'm fine." I lie.

"Rose, you're about to cry. You need to go relax."

"No." I say stubbornly.

He shifts them both in his arms, and their cries fall silent. He pops pacifiers in each of their mouths and sighs quietly.

"How did you do that?" I ask.

He just shrugs, looking down at Liam and Logan.

I feel bad. How did he get them to stop and I couldn't?

"I'm going to go outside." I say, and I walk out before anybody can follow m e.

I sit on the floor in the gym, tears flooding down my cheeks.

How did Zane get them to stop and I can't? Do my babies not know who I am? Why the hell am I crying?

Is he a better parent than me? Why does he always make sure I'm getting enough sleep? He dropped out of football for me, and he sits back and watches it on TV, and I know he misses it, especially since the Packers aren't doing so well this season. The media is talking all about him, wondering why he left, wondering where is he and what he's doing.

People message him asking him how he could just abandon his team.

I feel like a horrible person, a horrible wife, and a horrible mother.

I shouldn't even have babies if I'm this horrible at it.

I hear footsteps but I don't look up.

Whoever it is doesn't need to deal with my problems.

"Do you want to talk about it?" Zane asks.

"No." I sniffle. "Go away Zane, go hang out with the guys. You deserve it. You earn it."

"My parents are taking the twins tonight." He informs me. I lift my eyes from my hands to look at him.

"What?"

"My parents are taking the twins tonight." He repeats. "You have a lot of breast milk pumped. They'll be fine."

"No." I say immediately. "No way. Hell no."

He walks over to me.

"You need to sleep." He says.

"You need to sleep!" I retort. "Fucking dammit Zane, you left football for this! For me! For the twins! You left your dream! I feel like a horrible wife, and the twins? How could you get them to stop crying and I couldn't? I'm their mother!"

He moves to stand in front of me.

"Rosie, I left football because I wanted to. I have a lot of dreams, football is one of them, and I did it. I want a family with you and eight kids."

"Zane, I'm struggling with two." I say seriously. "I don't even know if I want more."

"You want more." He says. He looks down. "Do you really not want more? I know you wanted two..." he trails off.

"Eight kids, Zane? That's absurd."

"Five?" He whispers.

I sigh softly.

"Five." I give in. "But not for a while. I'm not ready yet."

"Neither am I." He says. "Listen Rosie, you're a wonder Mommy and a wonderful wifey. One night won't hurt us without them, okay? One night, baby girl."

———

I study my body, and my lose skin is still there but it's going away.

I took a bubble bath and it has given mean opportunity to clear my head, and I know I need to have a talk with Zane, because this arrangement for us is not working out too well.

I wander out of the bedroom in my pajamas. He's not in the study or in the living room. In fact, he's not on the first floor at all.

"Babe?" I bellow.

"Coming!" He calls. I can't tell where he is, so I walk into the kitchen and pour myself a glass of apple juice. "Yes?" He asks behind me.

"Do you want some juice?" I ask.

"I guess. What's up baby girl?"

"We need to talk." I say, handing him my glass and pouring another. He thanks me, but I can see nerves on his face.

"Thank you." He mumbles.

"You're welcome." I reply. He looks super nervous, so I lean up and kiss his cheek.

"Am I in trouble?" He asks, following me to the table.

"Zane, you're thirty one years old. You're not in trouble."

"Okay..." he sits down at the table and I take the seat across from him.

"I made a list." I say, pulling it out of the waistband of my pajama pants.

"Rosie, we don't do this. Are you asking for a divorce?"

"What? No, of course not." I smile. "But we do need to talk, and I have a lot of things I need to get off my chest, and some things need to change." I push my chair back and prop my feet up on the table. He smiles a little.

"You have small feet." He says. I have on white fuzzy pajama pants with Mickey Mouse on them in black, and a black long sleeve t-shirt.

I smile at him and unfold the paper. He sips his juice and watches me. Tank enters the room and curls up on the floor beneath us.

"This isn't working out."

"What isn't working out?" He asks.

"You're getting a lot less sleep than I am." I say seriously. "You get up most times during the night and you don't let me help. You change diapers and only bring them to me and allow me to help when they need to eat. I feel as though I'm doing absolutely nothing and you're doing everything. Today when they were crying and I didn't ask for you, it was because I feel like I'm a horrid mother. I should be able to soothe my own children. This needs to change. You need to let me help. You aren't getting enough sleep. There are two of us. We can handle two ten week olds."

He looks so handsome as he watches me. He's sitting up at the table with his hands clasped together, his elbows on the table. His chin rests on his clasped fingers.

"Rose, you are getting less sleep than I am."

"No I'm not." I say.

"Yes you are." He says calmly. "The twins sleep six hours at night. They go to bed at nine and wake up at three, and then they go back to sleep around four. You wake up to feed them and I am up for the full hour, and then they go right back to sleep. They wake up again around ten, and then we're both up for the day."

"Yeah, but you're up longer for the night-"

"Rose, I'm not done." He says patiently. I press my lips together and close my mouth. He never interrupts me and he's very patient. I need to do the same. "Now, you wake up Monday through Friday and spend about four hours training with Amber, which knocks out all of your energy. You come home and feed the twins, you do the laundry, you make breakfast, you clean..." he pauses. "But I stay home and while you're doing your things, I take care of the twins, I change diapers and do everything I can do without you. When they nap, I nap. I get more sleep."

I run my fingers through my brown hair and sigh quietly.

"I want to spend more time with them, Zane. They don't know who I am."

"They know who you are." He says calmly.

"I think I'm going to stop training and work out on the side. It's all loose skin. I can do at home workouts for that."

"I don't want you to stop training if you don't want to stop training. Don't feel obligated to stop training."

"I would like to stop training." I say seriously. "I'll just go jogging and workout in the garage or something."

"Are you absolutely sure this is what you want to do? You shouldn't feel like you have to do anything."

"I don't feel like I have to." I smile. "I want to, baby. It's okay."

He smiles softly.

"Okay." He says.

"So if I'm home in the mornings with you now...I think we need to come up with some sort of routine."

"Wait." He says. "I'm sorry for interrupting you, but if you want more time with the twins, I would like more time to help you do things. I can do the laundry or something."

"Alright." I stand up from the table and walk over to the junk drawer in the kitchen. I grab a pen and walk over to my list, flipping it over.

"What are you doing?" He wonders.

"Making a list of everything that needs done around the house."

"Okay." He says.

"Okay, laundry, folding laundry, cleaning the kitchen, vacuuming, sweeping, cleaning the bathrooms, taking out the trash in the house and also to the street on Thursday's. Um..."

"Cooking." He says.

"Yes, cooking." I nod.

"Dusting." He adds. "And you can go ahead and throw salting the driveway because I feel like this might be a long and bad winter."

"Okay, dusting, salting...grocery shopping."

"Right."

I keep writing things down.

"Okay, salting the driveway will be every now and again...and shoveling, I have to add that." I snap my fingers and add it to the list. "Okay, shoveling, taking the trash out, dusting, grocery shopping...those are all things that happen once a week or less."

"Right." He says.

"So which ones do you want to do?" I ask.

"Erm...I'll do shoveling and the salt...and the trash. And the grocery shopping...well the twins can go out in public next month, right? When they're three months?"

"Yes."

"Okay, well for the rest of that time I'll do it and then after when they can do we'll all do it unless we can't, okay?"

"Okay." I nod, agreeing.

"I'll do dusting and the bathrooms and clean, because I'm picky about those things.

He nods in agreement.

"Do you want to split cooking?" I ask. "Like one day I make breakfast and lunch and you make dinner, and the next day you make breakfast and lunch and I make dinner?"

"Yes." He says. "And we can clean the kitchen together. Like I can wash dishes and you can dry and put away?"

"Yes." I say, nodding. "I'll sweep and vacuum." I add.

"And can you do the laundry? Like put the loads on? I'll change them over and fold them, but I'm not sure the whites and colors and it's just confusing and I worry I might bleach the clothes or turn one of my shirts pink or something."

"How about I do the laundry all together and you fold it? Some things can't be put in the dryer."

"Okay." He says. "What about Tank? Who takes care of him?"

"Whoever gets there first." I shrug. "But I also think he needs to go on a walk twice a day. The entire day should accumulate to about a mile of him walking, so a quarter mile there and a quarter mile back in the morning and the same thing at night."

"I agree." He says. "Do you want to take turns?"

"Sure." I shrug.

"I'll do nights." He says. "Having you walking out in the dark like that makes me worried."

"Just promise me you will wear light clothing and stay on sidewalks please."

"I promise." He says.

"And now what about Liam and Logan?" I ask. "They are on a fairly consistent schedule and I would like to keep it that way."

I agree completely." He says. "I think we should just do it so when they need something, we just pick then. Having a schedule with them can be confusing and unpredictable."

I nod in agreement and write that down.

"Rose, if you don't want to quit training I can take on more responsibility."

"I want to leave training and focus on my family." I say. "I can get better without having to have a trainer."

"Okay." He says. "I would just like to mention again that you're beautiful the way you are and you don't need a trainer."

"Thank you." I smile, and I flip the list over.

"What else have you got on there?"

"Oh yeah. With the groceries, I want to put a notepad on the fridge and when we run out of something it gets put on the list. It'll be much easier than rifling through the fridge every Saturday looking for things missing."

"That's a good idea." He says.

"Also, my Mom wants to know what the deal is with Thanksgiving this year." I say. "Are we having it there? Should we invite everyone here? And Halloween? Are we going to my Mom's to hang out and watch movies or something?"

"Um...I'm not sure." He says. "What do you want to do?"

"Thanksgiving here means cleaning." I say. He smiles.

"That's what I was thinking. As for Halloween, our neighborhood is very stretched out and I don't think we're going to have many kids. We should get the kids costumes and go to your parents house."

"I agree. What about your parents?"

"Well I'm sure Alice is going out. I don't know."

"Also, are we going to have pumpkin carving here or at my Mom's?"

"At your Mom's for the same reason we're having Thanksgiving over there."

I chuckle and nod in agreement. "Does that make us bad people?"

"No, it makes us young parents of two infants who have a lot of other things to do instead of cleaning up after other people."

"True." I nod. "Okay, and Christmas. What are we going to do?"

"I want to start a tradition where the boys get pajamas on Christmas Eve. Our other kids can do it too. They get a new pair of pajamas to sleep in and wake up in on Christmas morning. Isn't that so cute?"

"Yes." I smile. "We can do that. But do you want to sleep here? Usually we sleep at my Mom's."

"I want to sleep here. It's not just us anymore, and the kids should be able to celebrate here."

"I agree." I say. "Are we going to make them lists?"

"Sure. We can make lists of what they're going to need in the future."

"Okay." I write that down also and sip my juice. "I think that was it." I glance up at him, 'Want to add anything?" I take another sip of my juice and study him.

He hesitates, glancing down at his hands.

"I um..." he bites his lip. "Rosie, I'm just a man, and I have needs."

I frown. "We had sex this morning."

He traces the wood on the table with his fingernail, a frown on his face.

"I'm not talking about sex." He whispers. "All we do when we don't have anything else to do is have sex."

I pause. I want to say something but I don't, and then I remind myself that marriage is about communication.

"I thought that was what you wanted." I murmur.

"No." He says, and then he sighs. "Well yes, I love sex, I love your body and I love pleasing you, but..." he swallows. "I want to cuddle more. We stopped cuddling when you were pregnant because you just weren't comfortable and we have't cuddled in months. Every time I try, we can't. I need more Rosie time. I understand we're parents now but I..." he swallows. "I need m ore attention."

It makes me feel really good to hear him say that.

"Like the other week when I napped with the boys and you told me to go to bed...I wanted to stay on the couch because you were out there. I just want to be close to you. I need more cuddles, Rosie. We don't hold hands anymore, and if there's a reason the affection has stopped...I'd like you to tell me. I feel so emotional all the time Rose, and sometimes I just feel like crying. Are we falling out of love?"

My heart falters.

"Absolutely not." I say right away. "Baby, we didn't cuddle when I was pregnant because I was huge and crampy and it was very hard for me to get comfortable."

"I know that, but it's been two and a half months." He says softy.

"Yes baby, and we have two babies. It's new. We're navigating the waters. I love you even more than I did before. My love for you increases every day."

I move his glass of juice and sit down on the table in front of him, leaning down to kiss him. It's not really a sexual kiss, it's very gentle and loving, showing him how much I mean it.

I pull away and hold his face in my hands studying his features for a moment.

"I love you, Alexander Caulton." I murmur.

"I love you too, Rosabelle Caulton." He smiles now.

"You are very handsome." I add.

"And you are very beautiful." He murmurs. He kisses the back of my hand softly. "Are we done talking?"

"Yes." I nod. I pause. "Do you want to go cuddle?"

His whole face lights up.

"Sure." He grins.

We finish the rest of our juice and put our glasses in the dishwasher. He puts the soap in it and turns it on, and I tack the lists I wrote to the fridge and put the pen back in the drawer. He shuts off the lights in here and leaves the light over the stove on. I follow him and he locks the front door and turns the porch light on. Tank follows us to the bedroom and curls up on his bed. I shut off the ceiling light and turn on my bedside lamp. I climb under the covers and he climbs in next to me he lies down on his back and pats the crook of his arm. I settle into his embrace, throwing my right leg over both of his and putting my right arm across his chest.

He pulls my shirt up and traces patterns on my back. I shiver slightly and pull the covers up over us so they're up to my shoulder. I can hear evert breath he takes and every beat of his heart.

"I love you." I murmur.

"I love you too." He whispers. "Listen, I'm thinking about getting a new truck. I want to run it by you."

"A new truck?" I repeat.

"My ford doesn't have back seats and I know you don't want the twins in car seats in the front. Plus I'm worried the transmission is going to go out soon. It's shifting weird."

"Alright." I say.

"However, I would like it if you went with me to look. You are my wife, after all.

I smile. "I'll go with you. How about we wait until the twins are old enough to go out? Say...three weeks?"

"Okay." He says. "But I'm not trading it in."

"Why not?"

"First off, it's old and nobody is going to want it, and second, our sons were born in that old thing."

I chuckle. "Okay. Whatever you want."

———

The doorbell is ringing frantically, and I can hear two different phones ringing in Zane and I's bedroom.

It's four in the morning.

Zane is already sitting up, and I sit up in bed too, kicking the covers off and following him to the front door. He unlock it and rips it open.

James is standing there looking exhausted. Madison is with him, and two car seats rest on the ground with two very angry infants inside .

"We can't do it." Madison says. "They won't take a bottle, they won't stop crying. We tried everything. They've been like this for three hours."

"Why didn't you call?" Zane asks half awake.

"We did." James says, exhausted. "Nobody answered."

I crouch down and unbuckle the first baby, pulling him into my arms. My breasts ache painfully.

"I'm sorry." Madison says. "Really, we tried."

"It's okay Mom." Zane says over the sound of the screaming. "Thank you."

"You're welcome."

"You guys get some sleep." I chuckle. "You look exhausted."

"I have no idea how you guys do it." Jame grumbles.

Zane just laughs and picks up the two car seats.

They leave and I shut the door with my butt. I roll up the right sleeve of the screaming baby that I'm holding and see a birthmark.

"This is Liam." I inform Zane.

"Rose, you can go to bed if you want to." Zane says.

"They're hungry." I reply. I go into Logan's room and sit down in the rocking chair. I set up the pillow and remove my shirt. I adjust Liam on the right and Logan on the left, guiding their mouths to my nipple. They latch on and suck noisily.

Zane sits down on the foot rest in front of me.

They nurse for a while and just as I begin to dose off, their sucking changes and I can tell they're using me for a pacifier. I hand one to Zane to burp and do the same with the other one. I have Logan now, so Zane leaves for Liam's room. I still don't have my shirt on but it doesn't really matter. I change Logan's diaper and put on diaper cream, and then I put him in pajamas and rest him in the crib. I turn on the baby monitor and meet Zane in the hall at the same time.

"We make a great team." he says proudly.

Smiling, I kiss his cheek and follow him downstairs. We turn the baby monitor up and climb into bed.

———

I like this chapter. I think it's good to show how strong their marriage is and how important it is to each other that the other is happy.What to do you guys think?Also, I had a few people say that they want Vanessa to have a girl so that Liam and Logan can date their child, and I would just like to remind everyone that Finn, Rosabelle's middle brother, is the father to Vanessa's baby, which will make Alexander and Rosabelle's children first cousins to Vanessa and Finnigan's children, and that's incest.Just wanted to clear up the confusion :)~Sam

Chapter Sixteen: Snow Storm

Chapter Sixteen: Snow Storm

"Are you absolutely positive that your parents are okay with this?" I ask Zane, pushing the stroller further into the mall.

"No." He says with a smile. I stop walking.

"Zane!"

"I'm kidding." He smiles. "Let's go baby girl." He nods down the mall hallway.

"This is going to take hours." I say.

"It won't be that bad." He promises. "I'll push the stroller Rose, I want everyone to know I'm a father."

I move aside and let him push the twins in the stroller. I feel like people are watching us but it's probably because he's well known around here. He remains oblivious to the fact that everyone is watching us.

When we teach our cell phone company store, he peeks inside.

"Do you want to wait here or do you want to take them out and carry them so we can go in?"

It's crowded here and it's also the week after Thanksgiving.

"Um..." I hesitate.

"Let's take them out and show off our attractive kids." He says. "Okay?"

I smile. "Alright."

I notice a lot of people, specifically females, looking our way.

You have nothing to worry about, he's your husband, not theirs.

Zane hands the first baby to me and takes the second one, carrying our son with one hand. He steers the stroller into the store and pushes it out of the way of everyone. I glance at the two girls that are alone and our age that are looking at my husband.

"What are you looking at?" Zane asks, forcing his eyes away from the wall of phones on the wall we need to head over to. I look at him before he can notice I was looking, but his eyes are already on the girls. I look over there and see them waving flirtatiously. He smiles and waves back.

Does he not realize what they were doing?

He looks back and me and smiles, and then he leans in and kisses me right on the lips, putting his left hand on my cheek so his wedding ring is facing them. He pulls away and pecks my lips again.

"I love you Rosabelle Caulton." He murmurs. I open my eyes slowly, looking up into his eyes.

He doesn't make a comment about me getting slightly insecure about them, he just smiles and tucks my hair behind my ear. "Let's get Alice her phone."

I shift the baby in my arms and follow him deeper into the store.

"Let's get her a flip phone." He says. "She can text and call. She doesn't need instagram."

"Don't be stupid." I say. "She's going to be thirteen in April. She's old enough to have a decent phone."

"Fine. She can have an android."

"Zane." I sigh.

"You want to get her an iPhone?" He asks.

"Yes. She can have parental controls on it."

"Rose, what if she tries to watch-" he covers the babies ear with one hand and presses the other ear to his chest. "Porn?' He whispers.

"Zane, she's twelve." I say. "And if she does, she will have parental controls."

"Can you even put parental controls on an iPhone?"

"Yes." I say. "I checked on the way here."

"Fine. She can get an iPhone."

The worker walks over to us then.

"Cute kids." She smiles.

"Thank you." Zane and I say in sync.

"Are they twins? Obviously they are. That was a dumb question." She chuckles. "How can I help you guys?"

Zane clears his throat dramatically.

"We would like to buy an iPhone three please." Zane says.

The woman's eyes widen slightly.

"Uh..."

"She's kidding." I say. "A six." I laugh.

"But not a plus." Zane says. "And not an S either. Just a regular six."

"Okay." She laughs. "Are you opening a new plan or adding it to yours?"

"We're opening a new one." Zane says.

"We're adding it." I correct him. "We already have an account, we're just adding a number."

"Right." Zane says, and he looks at me. "I'm just going to let my wife talk. She knows what she's doing."

The woman chuckles.

"What color do you guys want?" She asks.

"Black." He says.

"Rose gold." I smile.

Zane sighs quietly.

"I'm sorry baby girl."

"It's okay." I smile.

"You two are cute." She laughs. "You both look really familiar."

"That's because she's an Olympian." Zane says. "Number one gymnast in the world." He smiles and kisses my temple.

"And he's the quarterback that made the Packers win last season."

"Oh wow, okay." She chuckles. "How many gigs do you want the phone to be?"

I pause. "She shouldn't need more than sixteen."

"Alright. I'll be right back."

She walks off and Zane turns towards me.

"She doesn't need more than two gigs of internet." He says. "And she can have one hundred minutes."

"She can have unlimited minutes and messages and two gigs of internet." I say.

"Fine." He says.

———

We shopped around for about three hours before the twins started fussing for some food and diaper changes, so we went to the car for me to nurse then and get their diapers changed and now we're back in the mall.

"Babe, they need to come out of there soon." I tell Zane. "They've been in that stroller all day."

"Let's carry them." He says, stopping in the middle of the wide hall between all the shops. We're on the second floor by Yankee Candle. I pick up the baby in the blue onesie and he grabs the one in the green. I dressed Liam in blue this morning so this must be him.

We start walking towards Macy's.

"Excuse me!" A voice calls. Zane and I both stop and turn around.

Lucas. Fuck. I pull Liam closer to me.

When he reaches us, he stops.

"Oh. Belle." He pauses, and he looks hurt, eying the twins wearily. He holds up a familiar white sock. "The baby um...the baby kicked it off."

I look down at Liam's feet and see one of his adorable little baby feet.

"Oh." I say. "Thanks Lucas." I take it from him and put it back on with one hand.

"They're cute." He says awkwardly. "Congrats...on the kids and marriage and the Olympics. I haven't seen you in a while..." he sighs. "Anyways, congrats. You deserve it."

"Thank you." I say.

"And you too, Alex...on football and stuff."

"Thanks man." Zane says. He shakes Lucas' hand and I notice and wedding ring on his hand.

"You got married." I say.

"What?" He asks. "Oh yeah." He clears his throat.

Is she nice? I think he deserves to be happy. Everything in high school was like fifteen years ago. I've moved on and I hope he has too.

"It's uh, Alyssa." He says.

"Alyssa Fisher?" I ask.

The girl that literally went after me and tried to ruin me again three years ago?

"Yeah." He says.

Wow.

I nod slowly.

"Alright. Well congrats." I say. I want this conversation to end desperately and I feel anxious and uncomfortable.

I think Liam picks up on that because he starts whining quietly and then starts full on crying, looking up at me with sad eyes.

I kiss his little forehead and look at Lucas.

"Well thanks for giving back the sock." I say.

"You're welcome." He says.

I nod awkwardly. Zane must know I'm uncomfortable too.

"Listen, Bella-"

"Lucas?" A voice calls. We all look behind me and Zane and see Alyssa walking over to us, coming out of Macy's. She has a bag on her arm and her belly is large. She's pregnant.

I take the distraction to move closer to Zane.

She comes to a stop in front of Lucas.

"I found this cute onesie." She says. Lucas clears his throat and drifts his eyes over to us. At that, Alyssa turns around. Liam has calmed down and now he's sucking his thumb.

I pull his thumb out of his mouth and give him his pacifier instead, holding it there until he has a good suck on it.

"Rosabelle." Alyssa says. "You have twins?"

"Uh...yeah." I say awkwardly.

"That's sweet. Congratulations." She smiles.

What?

Did she just congratulate me?

"Thanks." I say. She's clearly pregnant and very far along. "You too." I gesture to her baby bump. She smiles.

"Thank you." She says. "Listen, I know this is way late but I was a real bastard in high school and a few years ago...and I want to apologize. I'm sorry for everything I did to you. You never deserved it and if I could go back in time and change it, I would."

Wow.

I can see truth and real regret in her eyes.

"I forgive you." I say.

"You do?" She asks, and she looks shocked.

"Yes." I say. "It was a long time ago and it made me into who I am today. It gave me what I have today. In a way...thank you."

"Thank you?" Lucas repeats. Even Zane gives me a weird look.

"I learned a lot." I shrug. "If everything that happened didn't happen, I never would have met my husband, I wouldn't have the house I have, the family I have...I wouldn't have anything I have right now. So thank you." I smile a genuine smile.

"I'm not going to say you're welcome because I feel like it's wrong." Alyssa says. "But congrats on the Olympics. You must have been terrified."

"Yeah." I laugh. "But it's okay. Adrenaline kicks in and I just pretend everyone that's watching isn't there." I shrug.

She smiles.

"You want to go shopping together?" She asks suddenly. "I need to go a few places without Lucas. You have good taste and it'll be more fun with a girl."

I hesitate and glance at Zane.

"You can do whatever you want, Rosie. Lucas and I can go shopping or whatever..." Zane trails off. "I'm good to get along with, I think."

This makes me uncomfortable. I forgive her but I can't forget what she did, and I'm not comfortable doing that. I'm more insecure around the two of them than I am around anybody else.

My phone vibrates and I put a finger up, shifting Liam in my arms to pull it out.

Vanessa: your location on iMessage says you're at the mall. Go home bitch. Snow storm is coming and it's supposed to be bad. Roads are getting closed in the next two hours and cops are gonna ticket you if you're on the roads

We're in Milwaukee and the house is about a half hour away.

At the same time, my phone goes off again.

Mom: are you home? Do you have enough diapers? Snow storm is coming and it's supposed to be really bad. If you're not home get home

"I guess a really bad storm is coming and they're closing roads." I say.

"Snow storm?" Lucas asks. I nod.

"We should get going." Zane says.

"Okay then." Alyssa looks at Lucas. "We should go too."

He nods in agreement.

"Well it was good to see you." Alyssa smiles.

"Yeah, you guys too." I say.

She waves to the twins and says goodbye to Zane and then leaves with Lucas.

"Is there really a storm?" Zane asks.

"Yes." I say.

"Alright." He yawns. "Let's go home then."

———

I turn the monitor up and wander downstairs. Zane is staring at the corner of the living room with a frown when I walk in. He just got done salting the driveway.

"What's up?" I ask him.

"You trust me, right? You know, not to cheat and stuff?"

I frown. "Of course."

"Because my Dad fucked up Rose, and he knows he fucked up and he got help. I'm not going to fuck up."

"I know that, Zane. What's the matter baby? Where is this coming from?"

I sighs and sits down on the couch.

"Those girls were looking at me and you looked...insecure. As if you would expect me to have sex with them."

I sigh slowly.

"Zane," I start.

"I just want to know why you got all insecure about them."

In answer, I lift my shirt to reveal the little bit of loose skin left and the dark line down my belly.

"Look at this, Zane." I grab the loose skin. "I'm so insecure about it."

He stands up with a small sigh.

"You are beautiful. I couldn't care less about that. I wouldn't care if you were so big that you couldn't walk. I would love you just the same, but I would worry about your health. You are extraordinary. You are radiant. Nobody, and I mean nobody can compare to my Rosabelle."

I drop my shirt with a sigh.

He studies me for a while.

"Are you mad Lucas married Alyssa?" He asks. I know he's been wondering. "The look on your face when you found out..."

"I don't care." I say.

"Yes you do." He sits down on the coffee table and gently pushes me down on the couch in front of him. "Lucas Black is married. Alyssa Fisher and Alyssa Black. They're having a child together."

Hearing it out loud just pisses me off.

"Well..." I clear my throat. "They're a perfect match. I'm not sad or anyt hing...I'm just...I don't know. She's changed though and I do forgive her, and I do forgive Lucas, but that doesn't mean I like them, you know? Like if you forgave Alicia-"

"I will never forgive Alicia." He says.

"I know." I put my hand on his knee. "I know that. I wouldn't either. But if you did, theoretically..." I swallow. "You wouldn't like her still."

"Yes." He nods.

"I don't know. I don't like either one of them but they both deserve to be happy. They just...it pisses me off that he told her off three years ago and now they're married. I don't know Zane, I don't know how I feel about it, but I don't like it. I wish them the best. Really, I do, but I don't want to see them."

Zane is quiet for a long time.

"Is this upsetting you that I'm still upset about Lucas?" I whisper.

"No." He shakes his head. "Of course not." He pauses. "Can I ask you something?" I nod my head and wait. He grabs my hand that rests on his knee and kisses each one of my knuckles, looking directly into his eyes. "Do you think that Lucas cheated on you with her?"

I study our joined hands and sigh slowly.

"I don't know. Whatever Zane, it was a very long time ago and I'm very happy where we are now. Lucas will always upset me, and yes I've forgiven him but that doesn't mean I'm okay with him. I think I'm pissed that he picked her out of everyone. That's like a direct punch in the face."

"I'm sorry, baby girl." He runs his thumb over my knuckles. "You can cry about it if you want. I'm here, you know."

"I stoped crying over my high school life a long time ago. I won that battle and everyone knows it."

"Yes you did, baby." He murmurs. "You relax, okay? I'll be back."

"Okay." I whisper. He kisses my forehead and walks out of the room.

My phone starts ringing and I grab it quickly.

"Hello?"

"Hey sis." Finn says. "Can Vanessa and I come to your house to wait out this storm? We didn't buy any water."

"Yeah." I say because I know Zane won't care. "I'll unlock the front door. Be quiet when you come in though, the twins are sleeping."

"Okay." He says.

I walk over to the front door and unlock it, and then I wander into the bedroom.

"Babe?" I ask. I hear water running in the bathroom so I walk right in. We don't knock on doors we know the other is behind simply because we don't keep secrets. If I wanted privacy I would ask for it and so would he.

But when I walk in, he's sitting on the edge of the tub completely naked and erect.

"Are you masturbating?" I ask bluntly.

"No." He says.

"Did you walk out to masturbate?" I smile.

"No." He smiles too. "We're going to take a bubble bath, Rosie."

"So why are you hard?' I ask, pointing to his dick.

"Because I was thinking about the bubble bath."

"Bubbles and hot water make you horny?" I smile.

"No, but you naked does." He says. "We don't have to have sex." He adds. "But you need to relax."

I smile suddenly, and then I start laughing.

"What? Why are you laughing?"

"Do you remember that time you pantsed me at the old house and I wasn't wearing any underwear? Do you remember how embarrassed we both were? Now look at us."

"We're married Rosie." He reminds me. "And we've been together for a while. There's nobody in the world that I'm more comfortable with than you."

I smile and walk over to him, leaning down to kiss him.

"Vanessa and Finn are coming over to wait out the storm." I inform him.

"Why?" He whines.

"Are you mad?" I ask.

He huffs and crosses his arms like a child.

"No. He grumbles. "But why?"

"Because they didn't buy any water and Vanessa is pregnant."

"Okay." He grumbles.

I walk over to the glass doors and push them shut.

When we first moved in, out bathroom had double glass doors and you could see everything so we put a fog screen on it so it's fogged glass and you can't see anything unless you're like pressed up against the glass.

I lock the door and text Vanessa.

Me: Zane and I are gonna fuck in the tub so don't come in the room unless you need something

I set my phone on the counter and pull my shirt off, followed by my jeans and my bra and panties. His eyes are wide with excitement. I put my hand on my belly to cover the skin there.

"Don't be insecure. You're beautiful." He says. "I'm not kidding, Rosie. "Come here."

I walk over to him and he pulls my hands off of me and kisses my belly, and then stands up to kiss my lips. The tub is full of bubbles so he shuts off the water and turns the jets on.

———

After two rounds of sex and us washing each other, we sit in the tub. I heard Vanessa and Finn come in during the second round of sex and I made sure to be extra quiet which was a struggle because he really knows how to please m e.

He's rubbing my back and placing kisses on my skin.

I feel him kneading a tense spot. He's done almost all of my back already. I hear footsteps in our bedroom and then start knocking on the bathroom door.

"The twins are hungry." It's Vanessa. "I changed their diapers and tried to give them some of the pumped milk in the fridge but they won't take the bottle."

I hesitate.

"How log have they been awake?" I call.

"I dunno. Half hour? Forty five minutes?"

"Why didn't you come get us?" Zane asks.

"Because I wanted to take care of them." She says. "But I can't feed them Belle, so you need to come out here."

"Alright, I'll be there in a minute. Thanks Ness."

"Welcome." She says. He footsteps disappear.

After drying off and dressing and brushing my hair, I wander out of the bedroom to the living room where both babies are wailing.

"What have you been doing in there for so long?" Finn asks.

"Having sex." I say.

His face contorts in disgust. "That's disgusting, Rosabelle. Why did you tell me that?"

"Because you asked." I say, taking my son from his arms. I grab the body pillow and set the first baby on my left. Vanessa hands the second baby to me and I set him on my right so their bodies go behind me across the pillow. Finn looks away so I can lift my shirt but Vanessa doesn't because I know she doesn't really care. When they're both attached I pull my shirt over them.

Finn turns back around and Zane comes sauntering into the living room. Finn glares at him, but their relationship is like a close friendship or a brother friendship.

"What?" Zane asks.

"You were having sex with my sister." Finn grumbles.

"Yes." He says. "With my wife. You know we've had sex before, right? I mean we do have twins?"

"I don't want to know."

"Then you shouldn't have asked." I shrug.

"Well-"

"Finn, it doesn't matter. They're married." Vanessa says.

He huffs and looks away like a child.

"Guess what." I say.

"What?" Vanessa asks.

"Lucas and Alyssa?" I ask. "They're married."

That makes Finn snap out of his mood real fast.

"They're married?" He asks.

"You're kidding." Vanessa says.

"And Alyssa is pregnant."

"No way." Finn sits up. I smile.

I swear everyone loves drama as long as they don't have to deal with it.

"Wait, where did you get this information?" Vanessa asks.

"From my own two eyes. Today in the mall. And Alyssa apologized for treating me terribly, and then she asked me to go shopping with her."

"No way." Vanessa says. "No, absolutely not. I don't trust her for one second. She's probably trying to get you away from Zane so she can stab you with a fork."

"Why a fork?" I ask. "Why not a knife?"

"Because she's a crazy bitch and she can't find a sharp enough knife in the mall." Vanessa says.

"Actually, I think there's a cutlery place in the mall." Finn says.

"That's true." I say with a smirk.

"God, I hate her." Vanessa grumbles. "Also what does it mean if my stomach is hard and it hurts really bad?"

I stare at her.

"What?" I ask.

"What does it mean if my stomach is hard and-"

"Get up." I say.

She stands up.

"Move around a little bit."

She does.

"Did it stop?" I ask.

She frowns. "No. Why?"

Shit.

I glance at the window and see the snow is so thick that you can't see anything. Straight outside the window is pure white.

"Why?" Vanessa asks again.

"Belle?" Finn sits up.

"When I went into labor with the twins my stomach kept tightening and it wouldn't stop when I moved around and I thought it was just braxton hicks...but it wasn't. If it doesn't stop when you move around it's real labor."

Everyone stares at me.

"What?" Vanessa asks. "I...I have hardly any bump. There's no way. I don't even know how far along I am!"

"We need to go to the hospital." Finn says.

"We can't." Zane says quietly. "You can't even see in front of your face outside."

"Oh my god. We don't have anything. We don't have anything." Vanessa says.

"I could be wrong." I say calmly.

"But you don't think you are." Finn says, panicked.

"Everyone stay calm." Zane says. "Vanessa, you need to sit down. I'm going to get some things just in case you do go into labor."

"But we don't know how far along I am! What if the baby is dead?"

"Is the baby moving?" I ask.

"Yes." She sniffles.

"Then the baby isn't dead."

"We don't have diapers. We don't have clothes. Oh my god." Vanessa panics.

Both twins are done eating anyways so I pull them off of me and put them down on their mat on the floor for tummy time. Zane is out of the room already.

"Finn, watch them." I say, pointing to my sons. He looks scared as he moves to the floor to watch them. I walk out of the room and rush into the garage. We have an old box of newborn and an old box of preemie diapers.

I have a gut feeling that's my niece or nephew is coming out.

I fucking told Vanessa to go to the doctor the second she found out but she told me she was going to wait until after Thanksgiving. She found out over a month ago!

She's not showing much but there are stories of people who find out very late and she was having symptoms over five months ago.

I pray that my niece of nephew is okay and old enough to come out, and then I grab the boxes and drag them to the living room. I jog upstairs to the twin's closets where tubs of clothes that no longer fit them are, and I get all the clothes. I grab towels and baby blankets and the suction thing. I go downstairs to Zane and I's bathroom and he's ripping through the cabinets.

"What are you looking for?" I ask him.

"Rubbing alcohol." He says shakily. I walk over to him and grab the bottle right in front of his face.

When I turn to walk out, he catches my arm.

"Rose." He says. "If that baby is too young and we deliver it and cut the cord..." he trails off.

"I know." I whisper.

"What are we going to do?" He whispers. "If we deliver the baby and it's too young, it could die."

The power flickers and goes out completely.

Oh my god. The storm just started and the power is already out.

Thankfully the sun is still hidden outside so there's a little bit of light coming through the window.

"Rose." Zane whispers.

"Go close to vents." I whisper. "I'll start the fireplace and get blankets and flashlights."

"We're going to deliver that baby in the dark."

I just lean up and kiss him.

"I know." I whisper, and I walk out.

"Belle? It's fucking dark in here." Finn says. "I can't see the twins."

"Pick them up so they don't eat something." I tell him.

I hear my babies cooing.

"Okay." He says. "How are you doing baby?"

"I'm scared." Vanessa says.

"Me too." He whispers.

I take all the supplies I found and rest them on the couch, and then I walk into the garage and grab all the flashlights I can, flicking one on. I get blankets from upstairs and go into the living room.

Zane comes in after me.

"Rosie? Don't light that one. It's propane and we need to keep as much of that as we can so we can use the stove."

We have five fireplaces, so we all gather things and move into the room off of our room. I light the actual fireplace to get some warmth in this room. Zane walks out again. Tank happily curls up right in front of the fireplace.

"Okay." Finn says. "We need a plan. What do we do if the baby comes?"

We all exchange looks, the fireplace being the only thing illuminating us.

I hold the twins closely to my chest, both of them resting against me.

"Well?" Vanessa asks. "Am I going to die? Is the baby going to die?"

I don't know. I don't know at all.

"Nobody is dying." Zane says. His camera keeps going off as he takes screenshots. "Giving birth is easy. All we can do is hope the baby is old enough to come out."

"Am I going to scream?" Vanessa asks. "Does it hurt that bad?"

I just look at her.

"Yes." And then I look at Zane. "We need the scale and a measuring tape."

"Okay." He walks out.

"And the pop up crib please."

I hear him reply somewhere outside of the room.

"Finn, can you go get some tongs?" I ask my brother, shifting my kids in my arms.

"Tongs? Like food tongs?"

"Yes."

He looks terrified as he walks out.

A few minutes later both boys come back and Zane comes with the pop up crib in the box, wipes, diapers for our boys, clothes, the scale, and a measuring tape.

Finn hands me the tongs and I sterilize them with the alcohol and the scissors too.

"Now what?" Finn asks.

"We put up the pop up crib for the twins, set it up in our room and turn on the fireplace, and hope to god that the baby stays inside." I say.

———

Vote and comment!

~Sam

Chapter Seventeen: Drive Safe

- -

I apologize for the very late update. Writers block is horrid :/ALSO IF YOU ARE AN EMOTIONAL PERSON AND YOU CRY EASILY SO NOT READ THIS AT SCHOOL I REPEAT DO NOT READ THIS AT SCHOOL

———

Chapter Seventeen: Drive Safe

The moment the front door slams three days later, I hear Zane arguing on the phone.

"No, don't you understand I have two four month olds? I can't have cold water! It's December third. I can't bathe two four month olds in ice water!" He walks into the kitchen and angrily turns the sink on.

"Listen, I need somebody out here as soon as possible. I don't have time for this right now. I understand there's a list, but-you know what? I'm going to do it myself. There goes your seven hundred dollars." He hangs up and slams his phone down on the counter.

"Was that the guy about the water heater?" I ask.

He rakes his fingers through his hair and walks over to me where I'm nursing the twins.

"Yes. I'm so stressed out, Rosie. We're out of propane which means somebody needs to come with the giant truck to refill it. The wifi is out and so is the cable, and the hot water heater is broken and the guy who told me he would be here in six hours just called me and told me it's going to be six days."

"Six days?!" I ask.

"Yes!" He explodes. "And now the Suburban won't start." He drops his head into his hands and groans. "I'm going to have to take the truck all the way to Milwaukee to get a new water heater. I'm going to call my Dad and see if he can help me put it in. I mean, what is this bullshit? I can't believe the customer service! The twins haven't gotten a bath in four days and you and I in three.."

We usually bathe them every other day.

"You don't worry about the twins, okay? I'll take care of them."

"I'm going to go call my Dad." He mutters. "And take the battery from the Suburban."

"Aright." I say.

He kisses me softly and stands up.

"Are you sure you're okay with the twins?"

"Of course." I nod. "They're okay Zane. Everything is going to be fine."

"Watch, the heat is going to go out next. Maybe the whole AC unit will go out. Fuck this shit Rosie, I need a drink."

He walks out of the living room and grabs his cell phone. A few moments later, the garage door slams.

I grab my cell and dial my Mom.

It rings three times and stops.

"Hello?" It's my Dad.

"Hey Dad." I say.

"Hey Bells. What's up?"

"Is Mom around?" I ask.

"She's cleaning." He says.

"Listen, I need a favor."

"Sure kid, what is it?"

"Can you come pick me and the twins up? The hot water heater is out, my car isn't working, the wifi and cable is out...I need to give them a bath."

"No can do kiddo. Our hot water is out too."

I groan quietly.

"Alright." I sigh. "Thanks anyways."

We hang up and I try Vanessa but she's at home on bedrest. During the storm we made her drink a ton of water and lie on her left side. The contractions stopped and the moment the roads were cleared, Finn took her to the doctor. She's only about six months along. I don't want to stress her and Finn out. When I try Tanner, he sends me to voicemail and texts me he's working, and Reagan answers and tells me he's working. I try Madison but she's at work, and Emma is too. Since James is probably coming here and Alice is at school, that leaves one more person.

It rings four times and stops.

"Yes?" Mrs. Bennett's voice comes over then phone.

"It's your favorite athlete." I smile sweetly even though she can't see me.

"Hey Belle." She says. "What's up?"

"Are you working?" I ask.

"No." She says.

"Does your hot water work?" I ask.

She pauses. "Yes. Why?"

"You know you love me, right?"

"What's wrong?" She chuckles.

"Nobody in my family has hot water and I have two four month olds that desperately need a bath." I say.

"So come over." She says. "I haven't seem them since they were born."

"Oh, right...well uh, I also might possibly not have a working vehicle either."

"Oh gosh. Alright, I'll come pick you guys up. I'll be there in say...a half hour?"

"Great! Thank you so much."

"You're welcome." She says.

We get off the phone and I since the twins are sleeping, I put them in their cribs upstairs, carrying them carefully. I turn on their monitors and carry the other end around with me as I pack a bag to wash them up.

When I come downstairs, Zane is in the kitchen with the battery on the counter.

"Where are you going?" He asks. "And how are you getting there?"

He's a little snappy but I know he's really stressed out right now and he's not meaning to sound snappy.

"I'm going to Mrs. Bennett's because she has hot water. She's picking me up."

"How are you getting home? I can't pick you up. The truck isn't big enough for two car seats and you and I."

"I'll figure it out."

"Rose, maybe you should just heat up water on the stove."

I walk over to him and kiss him gently on his lips.

"It's okay baby, everything is going to be fine. I'm going to go to Mrs. Bennett's and I'll find a way home."

"Alright." He sighs. "Fine."

"Alright." I say.

He looks really moody and I just want to do something nice for him.

"Why don't I try to call the water place?" I suggest.

"It's a waste of time." He says angrily.

"I'll just try." I say.

Huffing, he dials the same number and slides me the phone.

I hold it to my ear and wait.

"Blau plumbing, this is Andrew, how can I help you?"

"Hi." I say. Zane gives me a weird look. After being married for over three years now, he's used to me bitching at people on the phone. "Um..." I fake sniffle. "I have two four month olds..." I sniffle. "And I can't give them a bath because my hot water isn't working." I start fake crying. "And I'm on my period and I think my sons are getting sick because I can't wash them and i'm scared to wash them in cold water because they could get hypothermia or something!" I fake a sob. "And my husband-he left me two weeks ago and I have nobody! Please! I need the hot water back! Please!"

"Well I can put you on the list." The guy Andrew says. He sounds flustered.

"List?" I ask, and I start faking sobbing even louder. "I-" fake gasp. "Don't have-" another fake gasp. "Time for a list!"

"O-okay." He says. "How about you give me your address and I'll be there within the next hour?"

"Twenty four oh one west cedar lane in river hills." I say calmly. "Thanks Andrew."

I hang up on him and hang Zane his cell phone.

"Somebody will be here in an hour."

"That was evil but so genius." Zane says.

"You should leave." I say. "He thinks I'm single."

"So? He's not going to come out here and leave because you lied." He pauses. "Can you do that with the cable guy too?"

"Sure." I smile.

I called Mrs. Bennett back and told her that I tricked the plumber into coming within the next hour and she decided to come over and hang out instead because her husband was driving her crazy. Zane ended up leaving to go take the battery for the Suburban to the store. Before Zane left, I called and cried to the cable guy and the wifi guy.

Now the plumber is in the garage working and I'm on the couch with Mrs. Bennett.

Zane walks in the front door with a new battery for the Suburban.

I took off my wedding ring and instructed Zane do the same if he comes home. He did though.

"You got the battery?" I ask him.

"Sure did." He says. "Is the guy in the garage the same guy you spoke with on the phone?"

"Yeah." I smile.

"Alright." He yawns. "I'm super tired."

"You should go rest." I say softly.

"I don't have time." He says truthfully. "I can rest later. The twins sleep through the night so I'll sleep tonight.

"Babe, if you're tired-"

"Rose, I'm not going to rest." He says stubbornly.

He grabs the battery and stomps out of the house.

"He's cranky." Mrs. Bennett says.

"He's having a bad day."

———

Later that night with the cable and wifi back on and the hot water heater working, I put the twins to bed and took a shower, and then I filled the tub with hot water and bubbles. I'm still wet and soaked from the shower, but I wrap myself in a towel and walk into the living room.

Zane is lying on the couch. He's been so stressed out and he needs to relax. He glances at me.

"Are you naked?" He yawns.

"Yes." I say. "Come take a bath with me."

He puts up a finger and waits for his yawn to end.

"I'm too tired for sex tonight." He says seriously.

"We don't have to have sex." I reply. "But you need to bathe and you need to relax. Come on, we won't have sex unless you want it." I yawn then from his yawn and he stands up and follows me to the bathroom.

"Rose, if something else breaks I'm going to cry." He says. "It's bad enough that we're out of propane. I can't handle another fallout."

"If something else breaks I'll handle it." I promise him. He tugs his shirt over his head with a yawn and sheds his jeans and boxers, cupping his hands over his groin.

"Why are you hiding?" I laugh.

"I haven't shaved." He says.

"So?" I smile.

"So it's gross. I'll shower and then get in."

"Alright." I shrug. "Zane, I don't care if you haven't shaved."

"Well I do." He says. "It's unattractive."

"It's human."

"Well...well it feels weird and I'm gonna shave."

"Okay." I shrug.

He walks over to the shower and watches me through the glass.

"What?" I laugh.

"Nothing." He blinks. "I zoned out. I'm sorry." He yawns again and starts the shower.

I sit on the end of the tub on my phone, waiting for him.

The scent of his shampoo fills the air and after nearly fifteen minutes he get out freshly shaven. He shaved his face too and then turns to me.

"See? Now I'm much more attractive."

"You never weren't attractive." I say. I stand up and my phone slips from my fingers, straight into the deep, very full tub filled with bubbles. The jacuzzi is on. My eyes widen and I look at Zane.

"Rose! Get it out!" He rushes for the tub and I clamber into the water after ditching my towel on the floor. I take a deep breath and dive under water, feeling around for it.

My hand hits it and I pull it out, coming up for air. I feel his fingers pushing bubbles off of my face.

"Is it broken?" He asks.

I look down at it and hit the power button.

"Fuck." He groans.

"It's okay!" I insist. "I'll go get it fixed tomorrow. My car works, right?"

"Yes." He grumbles.

"Tomorrow I'll get it fixed. I'll take the twins with me and you can lounge around the house."

He stands in front of me with his head in his hands.

"I'm sorry." I say.

"It's okay." He mumbles. "I'm so tired, Rosie."

"You can go to bed." I say helplessly.

"No." He says stubbornly. He takes my phone and sets it on the counter and climbs in the tub with me. "Let's sit in here."

I sit down on one of the seats in the tub and he sits on the other one. He sinks down so the water is up to his chin, yawning again.

When he stops, he opens his eyes tiredly to look at me.

"You are so beautiful, Rosabelle." He says. "I'm just looking at you and I'm like 'wow, this beautiful goddess sitting across from me is my wife.'" He smiles tiredly. "I'm such a lucky man. You make me so happy."

I smile, my cheeks flaming.

"Thanks baby." I murmur. "You're very handsome and there isn't a day that goes by where I'm not grateful for you."

He smiles brightly at me.

"Can I ask you something?" He mumbles.

"Sure." I smile.

"You told me you don't want any more kids." He mumbles, tilting his head to the side. "Did you mean it?"

I study him for a while and then I sigh softly.

"We can have more eventually."

"Eight?" He beams.

"Five." I say. "Maybe six."

He smiles. "I want two more boys then, and a girl. Maybe two girls. We'll see how our reproductive organs work together." He yawns.

"Why do you want so many boys?"

He shrugs.

"So they can carry on the Caulton name. So I can raise a ton of gentlemen and teach them how to be polite. So I can raise them to be strong and independent...so I can raise them so that if the person they have children with abuses our grandchildren, they'll be mentally strong enough to know and protect their baby."

It all comes back to his family.

"And I want girls so they can see what it's like to be treated properly. I want our girls to know how a man, how anyone should treat them, and I want the same for our boys. We're going to have respectful children who will stand up for each other. I want them to play sports, all six of them, just so they'll be active and healthy. I want them to travel during the summers with us and see how beautiful the world is, so they know there's more to live than technology. I want children who will have dreams, and I want to be there to see them achieve those dreams. I just want a huge family, Rosie. I want such a big family that our kids have to share rooms. I want our girls to look just like you, with your beautiful hair and your beautiful eyes. I want a huge family...and you know what else?"

"What?" I murmur. He rubs his eyes and yawns again.

When he stops yawning, he speaks. "I want our kids to see how we treat each other, so they can know what a healthy relationship is. We're not going to end up how my parents did. I'll never cheat on you, because there's nobody I could ever want aside from you, and I know you would never cheat on me. They're going to see what love is. They're going to have a great life. I just can't wait to share that life with you."

I study him for a while.

"Eight is too much." I say. "I don't want to carry that many children. We would have to move and I love our house. I think..." I pause, studying him for a long time. "I think six is plenty."

"We could renovate the basement." He says. "Turn it into two bedrooms. There's a bathroom down there. We could put Liam and Logan in the basement when they're older."

"Six." I say. "Eight is way too much."

He yawns, nodding slightly.

"I guess it is. When we were at the pumpkin patch before Halloween and all six of those toddlers were running around plus our two...it was a bit overwhelming."

"Exactly." I nod.

"So six." He smiles. "I can't wait until we have more. When do you want to have more?"

"I think they should be two years apart." I say. "So when Liam and Logan are one, we try again."

He grins widely. "Okay. And when the next one is one, we try again?"

"Yes." I nod.

"Great. I'm excited."

"Me too." I smile.

"We should get our tree soon. Tomorrow I'm going to put the lights on the house. Maybe tomorrow night we can go get a tree from the tree farm. Want to?"

"Sure." I smile.

We're both quiet for a while.

"Rosie?" He murmurs after a few minutes.

"Yeah?"

"I've been hard since we got in the water and it's hard as a rock." He smiles tiredly at me.

"So you want to have sex?" I ask.

"Good idea." He yawns. "Actually no. I-I'm too tired to thrust." He looks at me in his confident tired state. "If you suck I'll lick."

"Always blunt and confident." I smile. "I love you Zane. Really, I do."

"I love you too." He yawns. He's yawning so much that I want to send him to bed now, but I also don't want to, so I slide across the tub and pat the edge for him to sit on.

———

I'm going to be sick. That's what's going to happen.

I'm going to puke.

I sit outside of the hospital room in a plastic chair, my entire body shaking as I sob into my hands.

I can't go in there.

"Belle? What the fuck happened? He's in a coma?" Finn asks frantically. "A coma? Did I hear Mom right? Why are you alone?"

"B-because you're the f-first to show up!" I gasp shakily.

"I came as quick as I could. Vanessa is getting a wheelchair." He says. I feel his arm wrapping around me. I can hear the twins cooing in the stroller but I can't. I just can't. "I'm sure everything is going to be fine." He murmurs. "Everything is going to be fine Bella Bear."

"H-he was going to the m-mall." I sob.

"What happened?" I hear Vanessa asks. "Finn, is Alex really in a coma?"

Just the sound of his name makes me sob harder into my brothers shoulder.

I shut everyone out.

A coma. He's in a coma.

I can hear more family come but I can't go in there. I feel my Dad hugging me, my Mom, James, Colton, Tanner, Reagan.

Everything hurts. My whole body hurts.

We were just talking about kids last night. Last fucking night.

"Have you gone in yet?" Emma asks softly. I can feel her rubbing my shoulder and I just shake my head, my chin trembling as I try to stop another sob.

"I c-can't." I hiccup.

"You should." She says gently. "He would...if it was you. You just go in there and sit with him." She murmurs, tubbing my shoulder. "He needs you just as much as you need him."

I don't want to go in there and see him like that. What if I go in there and his heart stops?

"C-can you hear in a coma?" I hiccup. I look up at Madison. She has red eyes.

"Yes." She sniffles. This is the first time I've ever seen her cry. "Normal you can hear every single word. You can understand every word, but you can't reply. You can't move either, but you can understand."

"H-he's trapped?" I hiccup.

She looks down and nods. "Yeah."

"But he knows it's quiet." Emma says. "So you should go in there."

I look around the hallway at all of the doctors giving me pity looks.

"Fine." I sniffle. "But you guys stay out here until I tell you that you can come in, okay? I-I need to just, I need to be alone with him."

Everyone nods. I force myself to my feet and Emma rises with me. She puts her hands on my shoulder.

"You got this." She says. "You've got this, okay?"

I take a deep breath and nod, and then I force the door open and step inside, pulling the curtain shut before our family can see us.

When I turn around, my breath catches in my throat and I try not to collapse.

There's cuts all over his handsome face and a cast on his right arm. He looks like he's sleeping but I know better.

He looks pale. He looks sick.

Weakly, I scramble across the room and grab the chair. It scrapes against the floor loudly and I wince at the sound.

When I sit down, all I can do is pull my knees to my chest and sob against my knees.

I don't know how long I sit like that but I know when I look up, the sun is gone from the sky.

I stare at his face for a long time.

"I don't know if you can hear me but Zane, I'm so fucking mad at you right now." I hiccup."W-we were just talking about having more kids last night. Last night Zane, and now you're in a coma and I don't know if I'm going to have to raise Liam and Logan alone. I can't Zane. I fucking can't. You're-you need to wake up for me. You need to wake up and come home, because I can't do this alone." I start crying again, and this time I drop my head onto his good arm. He smells sterile and nothing like vanilla and m ints.

The memory of this morning before he left the house hits me and it takes all I have not to scream.

I hear a baby squealing in excitement and a little hand hitting my cheek lightly.

Mumbling a quiet "stop," I roll over in bed.

I hear another baby coo, only this time it's on this side, and a small little hand on my cheek.

What the hell?

Forcing my eyes open, I come face to face with the very familiar face of one of the twins.

What?

I prop myself up with my elbows and look around tiredly.

Zane is standing at the foot of the bed with a smile. There's a baby on each side of me

I sit up all the way and move each baby to the front of me.

"I'm going to the store." Zane says. "And the mall to get your phone taken care of."

"I thought I was doing that." I mumble.

"It's okay Rosie, I'll do it." He smiles. He climbs onto the bed and crawls up to me, kissing me on my lips.

"Morning breathing." I say, clapping my hand over his mouth.

"Hush." He says. "It's nothing I haven't tasted before. I think it's cute."

He pulls back and the scent of vanilla and mints lingers.

"I love you baby girl, and Liam and Logan."

"I love you too." I say, and I pick up the twins and make them wave with their little hands. "Say bye bye to Daddy!" I smile.

They both just coo adorably. Zane smiles.

"I'll be home in about an hour, maybe longer if I go grocery shopping now."

"Okay." I say. "Drive safe."

"I always do." He smiles. He comes back to kiss the top of my head and then walks out all the way.

"You told me you'd drive safe." I whimper. "You told me you were going to drive safe."

———

I'm crying so hard my whole face is red and I have to breathe out of my mouth why do I do this I don't get it

I am SOBBING

~Sam

Chapter Eighteen: Tears

Chapter Eighteen: Tears

I guess he got a subdural hematoma and had to get brain surgery with a scope up his nose. When he didn't wake in enough time they said he slipped into a coma.

Still, I've called five different doctors just to make sure all of them know what they're doing and they all tell me the same thing.

He had a hemorrhage in his brain from his head hitting the concrete. They had to go in and repair it and in the process his brain swelled which is normal and it caused the coma. They all told me that when and if the swelling goes down he will wake up. He could wake up perfectly normal, he could wake up and be awake but hot him, or he could wake up and be unable to move. He could wake up with memory loss too.

I'm hoping for the first one.

I cry a lot but I keep forcing myself to take care of the twins. Everyone helps me and they take them during the night.

"How about you go home?" Mom asks. "Get some rest?"

"Everyone keeps asking me to go home." I snap. "Stop asking me to go home. I'm not going home. I'm staying here until he tells me to go home. Stop telling me to go home. You don't know what it's like, so stop fucking telling me to go home. I'm not going home."

Nobody says a word and I turn all my attention back to Zane, silently praying for him to wake up.

He's going to wake up. He has to.

He's Alexander fucking Caulton for fucks sake.

He's going to wake up.

He has to, right?

Right?

———

"You know?" I mumble to my unconscious husband. "Do you remember that time when you came back from Washington? You moved here, re-member babe? And you gave me that massage and the next day I thought it was a dream? Remember that? Well I wish this was a dream." I look down at my hands, my eyes filling with tears. "I miss you, Zane. I miss you a lot. I'm lonely, and if somebody told me three years ago that you'd be..." I trail off. "Like this." I whisper, my voice thick with pain. "I'd probably punch them out...and you've seen me fling my body around a bar like a rag doll, so you know I have the strength to punch somebody out." I swallow. "I wish you would wake up and talk with me. I miss you." I study my hands. "I'd rather physical pain than emotional." At that, my throat closes up and a sob shakes my body. I pull my knees to my chest and grab his hand again . "With physical pain..." I sniffle and tears roll down my cheeks. "You can take pills and stuff to feel better. You can put cornstarch on a cut-don't ask how I know that-and you can stop the bleeding. But emotional? It's so much worse. It makes your entire body ache with a pain that can't be cured without the fixing of the thing that fucked you up to begin with." I sniffle. "I don't know if that makes any sense, but I hurt worse than I ever did in high school. I hurt worse than when you broke up with me. Sometimes I can't even cry, I'm just here. My mind is a fucking demon, Zane, and I'm so pissed off at the world. I was mad at you at first but it's not your fault. You're innocent in this. If you come out of this...well, I promise that we can have eight kids. We can have them, all eight of them. I'll give them to you. I'll give you anything, and I feel stupid for talking to you because I'm not sure you can even hear me...but I feel so alone." I look down at our hands. "But this time around we should go to a class to learn how to properly give birth and how to do an examination to know if I'm dilating or whatever, that way if I go into labor in the truck or something we'll know what to do...and we should keep rubbing alcohol and scissors and a clamp or something in the car. You know what? We could do home births. I don't like hospitals, not after this and after that nurse dropped that baby. I wonder if that baby is okay." I frown. "I wonder if you're gonna be okay." I sniffle. "My fucking heart hurts, Zane. Wake up." I cradle his hand to my face and cry against it. "Come back to me." I whimper. "Please."

Nothing. No movement. I feel so alone.

I drop my head against the side of his bed and cry. I rest his hand on his belly and cry hysterically until I can't anymore.

"I hope you know-" I cut off with a gasp. "That I'm aware this is my f-fault." I sniffle. "If I didn't drop my p-phone in the tub, you wouldn't have h-had to go to the mall." I hiccup. "And nobody gets it, Zane. Nobody understands. I just n-need you to wake up right now. You need to wake up right n-now."

But the room is silent and my heart drops even further. I cry harder, gripping the sheets.

"I'm so fucking tired of crying." I whimper against the sheet. "Just wake up, Zane. Right now. Just do it." I lift my head to look at him. "Just wake up." I whisper.

He doesn't move.

"I'm just going to go pee." I sniffle. I place a soaking wet kiss on his cheek and walk into the bathroom.

I look like shit. My hair is a mess, my face is swollen and red and tears are slipping down my cheeks.

I do my business and wash my hands after flushing and then walk back into the room.

He's still in the exact same position.

I drop down into my chair with a sigh.

"I'm tired." I mumble to him. "Emotionally, physically, mentally...I just want you to wake up so we can cuddle."

I drop my head onto his mattress again. The sheet is wet from my tears.

I let a few more tears roll down my cheeks and shut my eyes.

————

I sat there like that for hours until I fell asleep, and just now waking up, I can feel fingers running softly through my hair and my eyes fill with tears because I know the person that's touching me isn't who I want it to be.

I don't want to cry anymore. I want him to just wake up. It's only been three days and to me it feels like centuries.

I feel exhausted knowing I sat there and cried for hours before I fell asleep. I even moved his arms to be under my head so I could cry on him.

I just want him to come back to me.

I lift my head and see my Mom sitting beside me. I know she's upset.

Who isn't upset? Alexander Caulton is in a coma.

Saying it like that makes me want to cry.

I run my fingers through my hair and it just feels greasy.

Mom sighs quietly.

"Bella," she starts.

"I'm not going home."

"I wasn't going to say that." She says. "But-"

"I'm not leaving Zane."

"Belle, Zane is awake." Dad says.

My eyes snap over to the hospital bed, which is empty. I stand up.

"Where is he? Is he okay?"

"He's in for a CT to check his brain. The doctor said everything looks good so far and that he might be able to go home on Wednesday.

It's Thursday. The accident was Monday.

"Okay." I say slowly. "Why didn't anybody wake me?"

"He specifically asked us not to wake you." Madison says.

"Why?" I sigh, frustrated. "How long has he been up for?"

"Apparently since four." Dad says.

"Well what time is it?"

"Eight." James says.

I don't understand why he didn't wake me up.

"You promise he's awake and this isn't come cruel joke?" I mumble.

The door to the room opens and a nurse comes in, pushing my husband who's in a wheelchair.

He's rolling a bottle of water between both hands.

He's awake. He's alive and awake.

He glances up at me and smiles.

"Hey Rosie, long time no see."

———

I love him so much

~Sam

Chapter Nineteen: Stubborness Explained

Chapter Nineteen: Stubborness Explained

"He said four to six weeks." Zane argues. "I feel fine, Rose. I'm fine."

"No. Absolutely not." I say.

"Why?!" He raises his voice in frustration.

"I'm so sick of having this fight with you, Alexander." I seethe. "It's every day! Every single day! 'Rose, let me go to the store' 'Rose, I'm fine, I can go get your new phone' 'Rose, I'm going to go look at trucks so I can drive the babies around.'" I pause. "Rose this, Rose that." I slam the dish towel down my kitchen counter. "I'm fucking done arguing with you about it!"

"Then let me to go to the store!" He explodes. "You're being unrealistic!"

Our entire family is at our house for the day before Christmas Eve. We're having the holiday here since it's easier with him being ill and all. He got out of the hospital six days after he woke up and both of us were specifically told that he can get up and walk around but he can't be up for long, he can't drive, and if he leaves the house he needs to be in a wheelchair in the store.

The doctor said that this needs to stay this way until he says otherwise.

"You got out of the hospital four days ago!" I yell at him. "Four days!" I hold up four fingers. "You're not fucking going out!"

"I'm going stir crazy! I can't do anything! I feel fine!"

"Quit bitching!" I snap. "I sat in the house for four months straight! Four fucking months, Alexander! You've been sitting around for four days!"

Our family comes over a lot to see how he's doing and help me the best they can and since he got out, we've had this fight every single day. They used to butt in but last time Madison tired to say something to her son, he told her that if she didn't stay out of his relationship, he would kick her out.

"You sat in the house for four months because you let yourself get stressed out! That was your fault!"

I want to slap him across the face right now. I'm so done with this fucking argument.

"You know what?" I say finally. "Go get dressed. We're going to leave."

His face lights up.

"Really?"

"Yeah. Get dressed."

He practically skips to the bedroom.

"You heard the doctor." Madison says.

"I'm taking him to a fucking rehab." I say. "And they can help him heal."

She pauses, and then she looks impressed.

"Can you guys keep the twins? I'll be gone for an hour tops."

"Sure." Mom says.

Zane comes skipping over to me like a giant child about to go to the candy store. I grab my purse and the keys to the car and walk out.

———

"Why are we at a rehab?" He asks.

He spent the entire ride with his face glued to the window.

"It's an errand I have to run. Come on."

He gets out without argument and I walk to the door and rip it open.

He follows behind me.

"How about you sit?" I offer.

He drops down without argument.

I walk up to the desk.

"How can I help you?" The woman asks.

"Do you guys like...help people that have been injured heal?" I wonder.

"Sure." She nods.

"My husband...he's in the gray shirt, don't look at him because I don't want him to know why he's here." I sigh. "He had brain surgery. He went into a coma. He woke and was in the hospital for six days. He got released after his doctor told both of us he can't be out doing things, he can't drive...we have twin boys and they're only four months old. I'm balancing the world on my shoulders and he argues with me every day for me to let him shovel the driveway or go grocery shopping or car shopping. I can't walk around wondering if he's going to get hurt and fall into another coma and not wake up this time, so can he be admitted? Maybe just for a few hours or a night? Just enough to scare him into listening to the doctor?"

"Sure." She nods.

———

He got out of it. Of course he did. The doctors made him go sit through an hour long therapy session.

He's Alexander Caulton. Of course he talked his way out of it.

When he came out, he didn't even glance in my direction, he just walked right to the doors and went to the car.

The half hour ride home was silent, and he went into our bedroom and packed a whole suitcase, and then he went into the basement and hasn't come out since.

Three hours ago a pizza guy came to the door with delivery instructions to take the food to the basement and not to me.

He apparently described me to the man so much to the point where the man knew my bra size.

I had to convince our family that it was okay to leave.

They don't need to deal with this.

They left eventually and now I'm lying in bed, staring at the ceiling.

I can't do this. I can't go to bed like this.

Taking a deep breath, I grab the baby monitor and slip down the basement stairs.

I hear the TV and when I peek my head around the corner I see him lying on the couch with his arms behind his head. He's staring at the ceiling instead of the screen.

When my foot hits the last stair, it creaks.

He shuts the TV off right away and turns his head.

We stand like that for nearly a full minute, with him just staring at me.

There's so much anger in those eyes.

I can't fight anymore. I can't.

"Yes?" He asks. There's a sharp edge to his tone and I flinch.

I just want to know that he's okay.

I search for words but I can't find any.

"What do you want?" He sighs, standing up.

"Do you have trash?" I mumble.

"You're not down here to take trash, Rosabelle." He folds his arms over his chest and stares at me.

He's being very curt.

"Listen," I start.

"You tried to send me to rehab." He says. "Rehab. You tried to send me to fucking rehab. I'm not-" he cuts off. I swallow the lump in my throat. I don't want to cry, especially not in front of him, because honestly I don't think he would care if I did. "Don't cry." He sighs, annoyed. "I listened to you cry every night for days."

I bite my lip and look down, pulling my sweater tighter around my body.

It's warm and it reminds me of the affection that he's not giving me.

"You walked out of the bedroom, left your wife and kids at home, you kissed me goodbye and you left. Three hours later I got a phone call telling me you were in brain surgery. By the time I got to the hospital, you were in a coma." A tear slides down my cheek and I wipe it. "I thought you were going to die."

"Because you did't have any fucking hope. You didn't have any faith in me!"

"I'm not fighting with you." I say. "I won't do it. I don't feel bad for trying to take you to rehab."

"Of course you fucking don't." He grumbles.

"I understand you're having a hard time being trapped in the house, and while I was on bedrest I was snappy, but I wasn't a fucking cunt." I'm mad now. "And you know what, Alexander? You're being a fucking cunt. I'm running around taking care of the house and the twins and fighting with you until my throat is raw from screaming. What if it was me? What if it was me that fell into the coma? What if it was me that was refusing to listen to the doctor and risking falling back into a coma every day? A coma that I could die in? You fucking try it, Zane. You sit there and think about it. I can't stay here and watch you do this. I can't stay here and let you treat me like shit because I'm trying to take care of you. You're a grown ass man. You want to do everything yourself? Go right ahead. I'm leaving."

"You're lying." He snaps. "You're not leaving."

My facial expression doesn't change.

"I can't sit around and watch you do this to yourself. I can't sit around and be treated like this."

"You tried to put me in rehab!" He exclaims.

"You've been treating me terribly since before that!" I snap, stepping off the bottom step so I'm fully in the basement. "You were in a coma, you idiot! You could have died! You had brain surgery less than two weeks ago! Yeah, I cried. I cried because I love you and I thought you were going to die! I can't do it, Zane! I won't!"I walk towards the steps.

"Don't leave." He says.

"Why do you even want me to stay?" I ask angrily. "Because you know if I leave the twins come with me, or do you want me to stay because I'm me?" I ask.

"I-I-"

"The fact that you have to think about that-"

"-It's not that-"

"–is ridiculous, and-"

"I don't know you!" He cuts me off once and for all.

"What the fuck do you mean you don't know me?" I laugh humorlessly. "What the fuck happened to you?"

"I don't remember you." He whispers weakly.

What?

"What?" I ask. My voice is calm now.

"I don't remember you." He says.

"You're lying." I say immediately. "You're fucking lying. You walked right into the hospital room and you called me Rosie. You-"

"I heard you talking when I was in the coma." He says. "A-and...I don't know. I don't know!" He runs his fingers through his hair and drops down onto the couch.

I slowly walk over to him but I keep my distance.

"But you told everyone not to wake me."

"Because I heard you talking and I knew you weren't sleeping." He mumbles.

"But you called me Rosie!"

"I asked my Mom what I called you. Her and Dad and Alice, they're the only one's I recognized...and Colton. I have no recollection of you at all, but I..." he swallows. "I got attached to you. God, this is weird. I'm your fucking husband."

I sit down on the coffee table slowly.

"So you asked your Mom what you call me." I say.

"Yes." He looks up at me. "And the doctor said my scans were normal."

"So the past few days-"

"I've been trying to take the car so I can go to the doctor." He says slowly.

"Why didn't you tell me? Or your Mom?"

"Because you..." he looks up at me now. "Because you really love me, and you seem sweet. I didn't want to hurt you."

Yesterday I was giving the twins a bath and he called Logan Liam, even though Liam's right arm showed his birth mark.

He called me Belle two days ago. When we sleep, he doesn't touch me.

"Do you know where you live?" I ask slowly.

"No. I-I know I live in this house but I don't know where."

"Wisconsin." I say. My eyes fill with tears. "You live in Wisconsin." I swallow. "Earlier when we were fighting and I said something about bedrest-"

"I found the medical file in the garage." He says.

"And you told the pizza guy my bra size."

"I went through your drawers."

I rub my face with both hands and let them drop to my thighs.

"So you don't know me? You don't know me at all? Do you know my middle name? How we met?"

He just looks at me. "I'm sorry."

The man sitting in front of me is Alexander Caulton.

This is not Zane. This is not the man I married. This is not the man that delivered our sons on the side of the interstate.

This is a stranger.

"I know you're an Olympian." He points to the wall of my medals. "Was I there for that?"

"Yes." I say. I feel so numb.

"Can I ask you something or a lot of something's?"

No matter what, this is still my husband.

The memories are buried somewhere. There's nobody better to help bring them to surface than me. I'm not going to run. Not matter how bad it hurts I'm going to stay and suffer with him. He's suffering so badly and he doesn't even know it.

"My um...Mom." He swallows. "She's alive?"

"She faked her death." I say quietly. "Well not really. She paid some guys to go tell you guys she was dead and then she changed her name and moved to New York and went to rehab. The only person who knew was Aunt Mia."

He studies his hands. His right arm is in the cast and he stares at it for a while.

"Look..." he swallows. "I really don't want you to leave, okay? Because I really want to remember you. I don't want to not be me. I want to remember."

"I'll help you." I murmur.

He swallows.

"What if I never remember?"

I study him for a long time.

"Then I'll make you fall in love with me again." I whisper.

———

K I'm sad

~Sam

Chapter Twenty: Bridges

Chapter Twenty: Bridges

Christmas was terrible. Everyone was informed the truth about Zane's health the next day and he kind of migrated near Colton and his family because he didn't know the rest of us.

He tried to help me with the twins and I know he really wanted to and I did let him because he wants to help, but it's not the same.

I feel like I'm cheating on my husband.

I keep crying every time I'm alone. The doctor put him in therapy and did tests on his brain and he said it might all come back or it might not. He said he might get bits and pieces and that's it. He also said he might get nothing back.

I'm hoping for the first one but I'll take the second.

He's stopped fighting with me about going out now and I find myself covering myself up when I'm nursing because it's just awkward.

It feels like I'm living with a stranger, but he's not a stranger.

He tries to remember and I'm not sure how to help him.

I've though about taking the twins and leaving him but I can't. I can't do it.

This is the hardest thing I've ever had to do.

He asks me weird questions sometimes and they'll be out of the blue.

The only good thing that has come out of this is me working out so much that I tightened up the rest of the loose skin.

"I have a question." He says. It's already January fifteenth.

"Ask away." I say quietly, flipping through the cookbook for something to make with stuff we already have.

"Did we lose our virginity to each other?"

My eyes snap up at his, startled.

Why is he thinking about that?

"Yes." I say slowly.

"I don't want to make you uncomfortable." He says slowly.

I push my glasses up on my nose and set the cookbook down on the bar top with a slow sigh.

"You broke up with me that night." I say. "I think it was a Thursday night. I didn't want to have sex until I finished with the Olympics because I didn't want to get pregnant and ruin my career." He leans against the counter and listens intently. "Anyways, you broke up with me because you were pissed off because Alicia showed up." At the mention of Alicia, his face floods with disgust. "I know you hate her. I hate her too." He nods and waits for me to continue. "And we would do other stuff involving...hands...and mouths." I clear my throat. "But we never had sex...and that night...well it felt right that night, so I told you we didn't have to stop..." I pause. "So we didn't stop."

"What were you wearing?" He asks.

"Uh..."

"I'm not asking for pleasure." He says suddenly. "I'm asking because little details might help."

"I honestly don't remember." I say truthfully. I take a sip of my coffee to calm myself down.

"Have we ever done anal?" He asks.

I start choking, spluttering coffee all over his white t-shirt and the counter. I turn on the faucet and gulp water, straightening up to look at him with wide eyes. The water I was gulping as soaked my shirt, making my white tank top see through. We both look down at my chest at the same time and my nipples are so noticeable that it's like I'm not wearing a shirt at all. I clamp my hand over my chest.

"I'm sorry." He says.

"We have not done anal." I say.

He squirms a little bit.

"Why not?"

"Because."

"Because why?"

"Because when you tried to stick it in my ass, I told you that you could stick it in if I could stick a dildo in yours."

"Why the hell would I let you stick a dildo in my ass?" He laughs.

"Why the hell would I let you stick your dick in my ass?" I retort.

He laughs harder and I find myself smiling a real smile for the first time in a month.

"Can I ask you something else?" He wonders when he's done laughing.

I nod.

"How did you get those scars on your shoulder? Was I there for those?"

He points to my left shoulder.

I open my mouth and close it.

"Um..." I wrap my sweater around my body so I don't have to cover my chest and swallow anxiously. "My ex boyfriend was..." I sigh. "This is a long story. You should sit down."

———

He didn't really say much after that, and he politely excused himself to the basement.

We both agreed that it makes us both too uncomfortable to sleep in the same bed, so as I lie in bed reading a book on memory loss, he lies in one of the beds upstairs.

Suddenly though, I hear knocking on the bedroom door.

Our room is weird. The bedroom door is down a hall and you pass the bathroom first. I hear the door creak.

"Are you awake?"

I shut my eyes for a moment to prepare myself for what he wants and then shut my book.

"Yeah, you can come in."

I hear the door open and close, and then he walks into the bedroom.

He hesitates at the foot of the bed, and them he climbs in on his side.

I guess the last thing he remembers is accepting the job in Washington.

He studies his hands for a moment. "I um..." he swallows. "Did your dog-our dog, Tank, right? Did he used to hate me?"

I pause. "No. Why?"

"I remember standing in the dark and something growling at me." He says. "I can see the face of the animal and it looks like Tank."

I think hard, my face screwing up.

And then it clicks.

"We were on a bridge." I say. "Remember I told you how you helped me after I got punched and I was rude?"

"Yes." He nods.

"I asked you to meet me at the bridge that night to apologize and I brought Tank. He was snarling to protect me just in case."

He presses his palms against his eyes.

"What were you wearing? I need you to remember."

I think hard about that night.

"Jeans." I say. "And a-"

"Tan sweater?" He whispers. His eyes open and they lock on mine. "Jeans and a tan sweater, right? You told me to be patient. I told you about Alice. I remember you asked me if she was my daughter, right?"

I smile. "Yeah."

He shuts his eyes again, his face screwing up in concentration, and then he snaps his fingers and springs up from the bed.

"I remember!" He points at me. "I remember everything before that! Rosabelle Caldwell, the English teacher." He says. "We got married?" He whispers, his hand slapping over his mouth.

I start laughing.

"Yeah. We got married."

"Okay, alright, so now my mind is caught up to that night." He says. "Now I remember Spokane and my genetic inability to make decisions. Jesus, it feels like you said that yesterday! We got married? Are you serious? I want to see a marriage license. I honestly feel like you're fucking with me right now." He puts his hand over his heart.

I run my fingers through my hair and stand up.

"Let's go get it then." I chuckle.

He follows me and I can hear him mumbling.

"Ms. Caldwell from three doors down is my wife." He mutters. "Holy shit."

I go to the fire safe box in the kitchen and get the key from the drawer.

"We're really married?" He asks, watching me. His eyes are alight with a flame I saw the day he walked into my classroom.

The man standing before me is the very cocky pro-at-sexual-innuendos-Alexander Caulton.

"We are really married." I say with a smile.

"You actually let me call you baby girl now?" He asks with a smile.

"I hated it." I say. "As you now know, but I just kind of realized you weren't going to stop." I shrug my shoulders.

"And we have kids?" He asks. "Two?"

"Yes." I smile.

"Which means we had sex." He says.

"Yes, that's how you get pregnant."

"And you let me have sex with you." He pauses. "Fuck, you did let me, right?"

My eyes wide slightly.

"You are a good person, Zane." I say seriously.

"This is weird." He mumbles. "I feel slightly uncomfortable but I'm also on cloud nine."

"You're on cloud nine?" I ask.

"Yeah. I married the hot teacher from down the hall."

I pull the marriage license out and hand it to him.

He studies it for a long time.

"I can't believe this." He says. "I'm going to go digest this." He holds up the paper and looks me up and down. "I knew you had a nice body under those work clothes." He mutters, and then he saunters out of the kitchen.

———

Arms slip around my waist the next morning causing me to jump. I whip around in Zane's arms to face him.

"What are you doing?" I ask.

I'm wearing only his shirt because I thought he was still sleeping.

"I can't touch you?" He whines.

"Uh, no. Back up." I say.

"But we're married." He whines again.

The change in him from remembering the very beginning of our relationship is astounding. He's slowly coming back to me.

"I'm not kidding." I say. "Let go."

He grumbles under his breath and steps back to look me up and down.

He's in his underwear, which is a casual thing for us but he doesn't know that.

And he's hard.

He looks so happy though and I know I'm in for the time of my life with him.

"Come on." He says. "Doc said yesterday that I could return to normal activity. We're not strangers. You're not a stranger anymore."

He knows all about Lucas because I told him yesterday after he asked.

"You want to have sex?" I ask.

"Yes." He says. "It could jog my memory."

"I genuinely think it's not going to jog your memory." I say.

"So? Let's just do it anyways."

I sigh. "No, I don't want to."

"But-"

"No." I repeat.

"Okay." He says. "I'm sorry. I pushed a boundary. I didn't mean to."

He steps towards me and I back up until my back hits the counter.

I don't want him to try and kiss me on the lips. I don't. To him I'm the teacher from down the hall and to me, he's...

I don't even know anymore. He's my husband legally but mentally he's a man that I fought very hard against ever speaking to.

He leans down and kisses my forehead softly.

"I'm sorry." He murmurs against my skin. "I'll put clothes on. I'm sorry. I'll go take a shower and put on clothes. I'm really sorry."

He scurries out of the room.

I brace myself against the counter and shake my head.

I hate myself for having so much trouble with this, but who can blame me?

I hate myself for wanting to tell him we can have sex.

Obviously I'm sexually starved and he is too, and technically there's nothing wrong with it but it feels weird.

But I want it, I really fucking want it.

He wants it too, and he is my husband, and it's not like I'm a stranger to him anymore. He remembers how we met...

The twins are still asleep...

I look in the direction he went and then grab the house phone, dialing Vanessa.

It rings four times and stops.

"What?" She grumbles.

"Be a good friend and tell me what to do." I say.

"What do you want?" she mutters.

"Should I have sex with my husband who remembers me as the teacher down the hall? Because he obviously needs relief and I do too, and-"

"Has it been more than a week since your clit has been touched?"

"It's been more than month."

"Fuck dude, go have sex. I'm going back to bed."

She line clicks.

Well Vanessa said it's okay...

I tiptoe down to the bathroom. Every bathroom in our house is connected to another bedroom.

I slip into the bathroom through the other guest bedroom.

He's leaning against the counter with his head in his hands.

I shut the door without turning the knob so it clicks shut, and he looks up at me.

He's still hard and I know he's struggling.

"What?" He asks a little bit harshly. "I'm sorry. That was rude." He sighs. "What's wrong? Is somebody here? Do you need me to get the door or something?"

"No." I say.

"Then what's the matter?"

The shower in here is small.

"Um..." I sigh.

This feels wrong.

"Never mind." I turn back for the door but right as I open it, he darts out and shuts it.

The way this bathroom is designed, the entrance is narrow.

Right now, I'm cornered between the wall and the shut door with my very erect husband who has no recollection of our married life or our sex life.

Our very, very good sex life.

"Should I have knocked?" I whisper hoarsely.

He seems to be completely aware that I'm cornered by he doesn't back up and I know it's because he's horny.

"Would you have knocked if things were normal?" He murmurs.

"No."

"Then no, you shouldn't have knocked."

Silence.

The shower is running in here, the bathroom is steamy.

I look up at him, my heart thudding in my chest.

I want him to press me up against the wall of that damn shower like he has before.

There isn't one room in this house that hasn't been broken in by us. We've fucked on every single counter, every piece of furniture, every tub, every shower, against every wall, on every floor.

We were newlyweds when we moved in.

His breathing is labored as he looks down at me, his eyes dark with an emotion that I recognize as desire.

"Why are you up here?" He whispers. "I always come to you, so why are you coming to me?"

If he remembered he could tell by one look at my face what I wanted.

"I've seen you angry." He murmurs. "Sad...frustrated, happy..." he swallows. "But not like this. What's the matter?"

He reaches up and drags his thumb slowly across my cheek.

I can't.

This isn't right. Having sex with him right now would be like his first time every, and in his mind he hardly knows me.

I can't do it for my own pleasure. It's not right.

"Never mind." I decide, trying my hardest not to burst into tears.

The more he comes back to me, the further away he seems to get.

"Are you sure you don't want to tell me?" He whispers.

"Yeah." I say. "Just try not to sing too loud. The twins are sleeping."

I reach behind me and open the door.

"How do you know I sing in the shower?" He asks.

I just smile sadly.

"Because I know you better than you know yourself."

I slip out of the bathroom.

I went to the kitchen and sobbed.

I had been trying my hardest to hold it in and I almost succeeded but then I was washing my hands and I touched the ring and I lost it.

Now I sit on the counter with my feet in the sink, my forehead against my knees, crying so hard that I'm worried I might puke.

How can I be so fucking selfish to do that? Of course he would joke about having sex? He's not Zane! He's Alexander Caulton! Zane didn't make many sexual innuendos like that, if he wanted sex he would flat out ask for it. He had no shame in asking me to give him head!

Alexander didn't mean it like that.

To him having sex with me would be him losing his virginity.

I hear the twins crying on the monitor and then they stop and I know he's getting them.

What if this is the only memory he gets back?

I could make him fall back in love with me but he won't remember the important stuff!

He won't remember the day we had sex for the first time. He won't remember that private moment when he asked me to marry him. He won't remember the day he found out I was pregnant. He won't remember me giving birth in the seat of his truck.

Nobody understands that moment. I have nobody I connect with more than him, but he's not here, but he is here.

I just want to go to sleep until he remembers.

That could be forever.

My attempt to slip into the bedroom is over. It's too late.

I hear him walk into the kitchen with two cooing babies. I hear him open the fridge without a word, and then he walks out.

He doesn't even care that I'm sitting here bawling.

I would give anything for the real Zane to remember.

Come back to me. Please.

I feel like he's dead. I literally feel like he's dead.

But he's not. He's here. He's in the fucking living room.

But he's not with me. He doesn't know me.

Suddenly, I feel his hand pushing my hair off of my face.

"I know you don't exactly like me right now." He whispers. "And I understand that you probably don't want me to touch you...but I can't sit back and watch you cry like this. At least tell me what I can do to help. I can go to the store and get you food. I can...I don't know. I probably did something when you cried. I can do that. So you just tell me what to do to help and I 'll do it."

I can't help it. I can't stop myself. I turn my body on the counter and wrap my arms around my neck, burying my head in the crook of his neck.

I feel his whole body stiffen.

Please. Please just hold me. Please.

I know he's in there somewhere, even if I have to recreate him and teach him what he did.

For a few seconds he doesn't move, and then I feel his arms wrap around my waist, pulling my body flush against his. He smells like vanilla and mints and the scent makes me cry hysterically.

That scent has been home to me for a very long time and it smells so fresh on his skin, and he feels the same and for a moment it feels like he's here with me and I just cry.

"I'm so sorry, baby girl." He whispers. He starts running his fingers through my hair the same way he has been for years and I cry harder. I feel him lift me off of the counter and then I'm laid down on the couch. He lies with me and he lets me curl against him.

The fact that I'm practically a stranger to him and he's still trying to comfort me just makes me more upset.

"Are you getting fed up with me?" He whispers suddenly. "Are you going to take our babies and leave? I really don't want you to. I really want to figure this out. I want this to work. I want to remember really bad. My heart hurts a lot. I'm really sad I can't remember. I'm trying, I promise I'm trying."

I lift my head to look at him, tears streaming down my face. I probably look horrible but I don't think he minds.

"I'm not leaving you." I sniffle. "We're going to figure it out. I'm not leaving."

———

I'm tired of crying

~Sam

Chapter Twenty One:
Three Weeks

C hapter Twenty One: Three Weeks

Alexander

I look down at the grocery list.

My wife has beautiful handwriting.

My wife. How strange.

This is all so strange, and I feel guilty. She's an excellent woman, definitely not the same woman I remember, but she's great. I can tell she really cares about me and the fact that she hasn't told me to screw off and taken our sons and left says a lot about her character. She's a strong, devoted woman and when I finally remember every single detail about her, I'm going to make sure she knows it.

I see tampons on the list and my eyes widen.

Tampons? I purchase those?

This is a regular thing for us?

I stop the cart in the middle of the aisle and stare at the list.

Tampons.

Okay, this can't be that hard. I do this all the time. I can do this.

I wander over to the tampon aisle .

Holy shit. How many boxes does one woman need? There's...there's twenty different brands, forty different sizes...

I don't know how big her vagina is! Do I get super? Is that insulting to assume she has a large vagina? I bet she doesn't, I should get regular.

But what brand? How many? Scented or unscented?

I look at the list and see her beautiful writing, hoping for some sort of description of what she needs, but all it says it the simple word. Tampons.

Why are they so expensive?

Okay, alright Alex, calm down. You can purchase tampons for your wife.

This is all so surreal and overwhelming.

Shaking my head, I grab two boxes super from Always and Kotex, three boxes of regular just in case she gets insulted by the amount of super I bought, and four boxes of small just in case she's little down there.

I look at the eight boxes and see none of them are scented, so I grab the same amount scented.

I'm a football player for the NFL and she's an Olympian. Our house is large so I'm assuming our bank balance is.

I throw my jacket in the shopping cart to cover the eighteen boxes of tampons and scurry through the store.

Diapers. What kind of diapers? What size?

I remember the two on the back of their diapers, so I grab a very large box of diapers that are size two and scribble them off the list.

I specifically remember Rose telling me to mark things off so I didn't forget anything.

As I roll into checkout I realize that everyone is going to see my massive supply of tampons.

I begged her to trust me to do the shopping. I can't disappoint her.

Feeling overwhelmed, I put all of my things on the conveyor belt and try to act like I don't know that people are staring at me. I hear somebody snicker near me and I feel my heart pounding.

I write down on the list to tell Rose to please explain to me how to properly grocery shop.

The cashier looks dumbfounded as to why I have so many tampons in my shopping cart.

Quick, think of a lie!

"My wife and I run a girls orphanage." I blurt.

"It's not my business." She says. Her eyes are wet like she's trying not to bust out laughing.

I watch as the price wracks up to four hundred dollars.

Can we afford that?

I run the card as debit and hold my breath.

Fuck! The code!

I hit the red X repeatedly and start digging through my wallet.

To my disbelief, I find five one hundred dollar bills in there.

The cart is loaded.

"Here, keep the change." I blurt. I push all five hundred towards the woman and squirm as she marks them with the pen and puts them in the cash drawer, removing the change.

"Are you sure? It's almost a hundred dollars."

"That's fine." I say. I grab the car and run for the doors.

I'm so mortified. I wish I could remember. The life that I used to live is a struggle to go back to and the woman I remember and the woman with the ring on her finger are two completely different people. I'm not sure if I can do this.

———

Later that night after the twins are sleeping, I walk towards Rose's bedroom, which is actually our bedroom, and I knock and then stick my head in.

"Can I come in?" I ask.

"Yeah." She responds. I slip into the room, my breath catching in my throat at the sight of her.

She's in a t-shirt only, my t-shirt, but it's long enough on her sexy frame that I can't see her panties.

Does she wear thongs? I wouldn't know.

"I need to talk to you." I murmur.

She shuts her book and sets it on her nightstand.

"What's up?"

"Listen..." I clear my throat. "There is a possibility, a very large possibility, that I will never get my memory back. It's already been over a month that I've been awake and I have no recollection of anything except for that night on the bridge. I go to the store and you send me this list like it's casual, and it is casual...but for you. I paid cash because I didn't know the bank code."

"I'm sorry." She sits up. "I should have gone with you."

"You're hurting." I whisper. "And I'm walking around surrounded by people that love me...and I don't know how to love them back because I know nothing about them." I sit down in front of her. "And I'm having a very hard time watching you cry on kitchen counters when I know it's my fault. This is all my fault."

"None of this is your fault." She says. "None of this is your fault at all. You're a victim."

"I've wanted a family for a very long time. My life here is-was-perfect, but the man you married is gone. When we go through the picture albums and I see photos of us over the years, you have this smile on your face." I put my hand in a fist over my heart. "And I don't, because while you're sitting there remembering, I sitting there wondering who somebody is in the background." I look down. "And it's not fair, Rose. I need to start over. Clean slate. I can't remember you, and-"

"Zane, I already told you-"

"You'd start over with me." I whisper, studying her. "And I want that, Rose. I do, but I'll be starting over completely and you'll try but when we're at the store and we run into somebody and they greet us like an old friend, you're going to know who they are and I'm going to stand there like an idiot. I can't sit around like this. You need to find somebody who can raise the twins. They're biologically mine but...but they're not mine. They're the man who helped you give birth to them in the car. I know you want him, and I'm not him. I'm giving up, Rose. I'm going to move out and file for divorce."

"Wait." She says when I start to get up. Her hand clasps mine. Her hands are rough but warm. I wish they were familiar to me. "Give me a chance."

"A chance to what?"

"To make you remember." She whispers. "Give me one month."

"I don't have any more months to give. I'm sitting around miserable all the time from how badly I want this life. I feel like a ghost watching from the outside. I can't do it. I'm depressed and I feel alone."

"Me too." She whispers. The sincerity in her eyes makes my heart hurt. I wish I could help her feel better. "The man you want to be...the man I want you to be...he's in there. Those memories are in there."

"I don't think they are." I whisper.

"I refuse to believe that. I absolutely refuse to believe that." She says. "There's no way this is the end for us. I refuse to accept it."

"I think you should accept it."

"Give me a month." She whispers.

"No." I say stubbornly.

"Two weeks." She bargains.

"Rose," I start.

"If you give me two weeks and I make you remember, you can have all eight babies." She pleads.

"What are you talking about?" I sigh.

"You want eight babies. Seven boys and one girl. I told you I wanted two and we agreed with five. I know you don't remember it but you still want eight. I'll give you all eight. Fuck, I'll give you eighteen. Just give me two weeks. Please Zane, I'm begging here."

I study her for a moment.

The man I used to be...he was a lucky man. She's beautiful and she's willing to fight for me and never give up.

"Please." She whispers. "Two weeks."

"Eight kids means that much to the real me?" I whisper.

"Eight kids means the entire world to the real you." She murmurs in response.

I study her brown eyes and plump lips.

"Okay." I whisper. "But you have to tell me the code for the bank. I want you to write down all the codes for everything..." I swallow. "And you have to kiss me."

"Three weeks then." She says.

"Two weeks is a fair compromise-"

"Either you get the passwords or you get the kisses. If you want both, you give me another week."

This woman is a force to be reckoned with.

"Three weeks." I give in. "But you better give me a good kiss. In my mind, this will be our first."

To my completely shock, she climbs into my lap. I'm in a thin pair of basketball shorts even though it's cold outside, and she's in panties and a t-shirt.

She looks right into my eyes so deeply that I fear I might pass out. She smells of shampoo and...god. She smells like god or something.

She takes her time to lean in and I can already feel the blood rushing to my dick.

The women I remember would probably freak out about my erection being pressed against her. Will she?

I remember that night on the bridge when I went in to kiss her...I wanted to kiss her so badly.

Now I get to kiss her, and while there's probably millions of kisses in between this one, it still feels like my first.

She gets so close than I can feel her breath on my lips. My eyes slide shut in sync with hers.

Gently, her lips press against mine, soft as first, and then firmer. Her lips fit against mine perfectly and I just feel warm all over at the feeling of her. Heat spreads to my body and goes right to my dick which is already swelling. I can feel myself touching something and I can't help and wonder if it's her.

Is my dick touching her-shit. She's in her underwear.

I want more. I deepen the kiss, my hands roaming up and down her sides. I could tell by the peaks of her breasts when we were talking that she wasn't wearing a bra. I notice she doesn't wear one unless we're leaving and I'm sure it's because she's breastfeeding.

She swipes her tongue against my lips and I open my mouth, our tongues mixing together. She tastes so good. My hands stake up and down her back, roaming lower and lower until they brush against fabric, and then skin.

I knew that she wears thongs. I find my hand reaching down to grip her ass in my hands. Her fingers slip under my t-shirt, sliding up and down my chest. She knows right where to touch me to make me shiver.

I want to take off her shirt so bad. I'm so hard that it hurts and I can feel it throbbing. I start lifting her shirt up and letting it drop again. I want to take it off. I really want to take it off.

Will she let me take it off?

The way she kisses is electrifying. It's not so fast that you can't keep up. It's slow and passionate. It builds up the desire and makes your skin boil for the person you're with.

I just wish I knew her better. I wish I knew if she would be okay with me touching her.

I want to remember so badly that it physically hurts to wake up and realize I don't remember anything.

I slip my fingers around the front of her, my fingertips brushing against the bottom of her breasts.

I start to draw back to ask her politely if I could touch her but I change my mind. I hardly know her, and if this is the new permanent me, I need to take it slow with her.

It's strange to know that she has so many memories of us in her mind. She knows every tiny detail. She knows things about me that nobody knows. She has more memories with me than anybody does.

This woman has seen me completely naked and I've seen her.

I want to remember so bad that it just ruins the mood. I pull away from her, running my fingers through her hair. She's so beautiful.

Has she seen me fully exposed and vulnerable? I know I hardly ever cry. If I do cry, I don't cry in front of anyone ever. Last time I remember crying in front of somebody was my Aunt Mia when my Mom died.

That's it. Nobody else since I was seventeen. In my mind, I'm twenty six.

But I'm not twenty six. I'm thirty one.

Did I cry in front of her? Is that a strange question to ask? Will I make her uncomfortable?

I don't think she would mind. I'm sure we talked all the time. Did we have good communication?

"Have I..." I swallow. She slides off my lap and settles back down in her spot on the bed. Her lips are swollen and I want to kiss her again, but it feels wr ong.

She's mine both legally and ethically, but she doesn't feel like mine.

I want to cry right now.

Did the real me seek comfort in her? She seeks comfort in me.

Do I go to her with everything?

"Have you what?" She asks.

She's so elegant and I watch as she brushes her hair off of her collarbone.

"Have I cried in front of you before?"

She raises both eyebrows at my question and I can tell she wasn't expecting it.

"What made you ask that?" She wonders.

"I don't know. I just...before..." I clear my throat. "I think that before you I didn't really show any serious emotion to anybody. Last time I remember crying in front of somebody was my Aunt Mia when my Mom died. I never tell anybody how I truly feel. Ever. I never have ever since I was a kid. Do we...did we have good communication? Did I talk to you? Have you seen me fully exposed and vulnerable?"

She looks down at the covers as if she's remembering something.

"I've seen you cry twice...but it was twice in one night, and the second time you were naked and crying."

I was naked and crying in front of her? Why?

"And you come to me with absolutely everything. You explain your feelings." She looks down at the comforter with a frown. "We had great communication." She whispers sadly. "Vanessa...everyone, they were jealous of how strong our marriage was. You and I..." she gestures between us and swallows. "We were inseparable. Nothing could wedge us apart." She looks up at me. "We didn't even fight. If you were upset with me you'd sit me down and we would talk about it. We never fought."

And there I was, coming home from the hospital and arguing with her to let me leave.

How badly I played her.

"When I realized I didn't remember..." I look down. "I should have told you right away."

"It's okay." She says. "You're struggling worse than I am right now. Everything is going to be fine."

I reach up and touch my lips that are still tingling from that kiss.

"You're a good kisser." I smile.

She chuckles sadly. "I learned from you."

We sit in silence like that for a long time. Eventually I lie down on my side and prop my head up with my hand, and she scoots under the covers and just looks at me, and I look back at her.

Is she thinking about that night that I cried naked? I wish I was.

"Tell me about it." I whisper.

I was fully expecting her to ask me what I was talking about, but she doesn't.

"It was the same night we had sex." She slides all the way under the covers and rolls on her side. I scoot further up the bed so I'm on my side and my head is level with hers. "That was also the night that you broke up with me and came back. You came to my door crying...telling me you had messed up. That was the first time I ever saw a man cry before. I saw my brothers when they were younger but I haven't in a long time." She clears her throat. "And after we had sex you started crying."

"I cried after sex?" I ask. "How fucking horrible."

She smiles at that. "You were crying and you were kissing me. Anywhere you could reach. My neck, my shoulder, my arm..." she frowns. "And you kept telling me you were sorry, you kept telling me how sorry you were and how much you didn't mean it, how much you loved me."

She looks upset now and I just feel guilty.

"I never meant for this to happen. To forget you. It's clear you meant a lot to me. Maybe everything."

That's strange to think about somebody meaning the world to me. Especially the English teacher down down the hall.

"I never meant to hurt you. I'm so sorry, Rose."

She smiles sadly.

"It's not your fault."

We sit in silence for a while again and I find myself getting tired.

"You need to pack a bag." She says softly. I feel her reach out and brush my hair out of my face. How loving. I hope I remember her someday.

"Why?" I mumble.

"Because we're catching a flight tomorrow."

At that, I crack an eye open.

"A flight? Why?"

"Because I'm not going to give up until you remember every single detail. I'm not going to stop even if it takes the rest of my life. We're going back to the root of our relationship. You're going to remember."

I feel her press a kiss to my forehead and then the light goes out.

"Are you going to sleep?" I ask quietly.

"Yes." She says. I hear her shuffling around.

"I don't want to get up." I murmur.

She pauses her movements.

"So don't get up." She whispers.

So I can sleep in here?

I open my mouth to ask if she's okay with me taking my shirt off, but then I remember she's my wife and she's probably seen me shirtless more than anybody.

I tug my shirt over my head and toss it on the floor, slipping under the covers.

I hear her stop shuffling around and then silence.

I'm worried this trip we're taking won't work.

If it doesn't work...

Well if it doesn't work, I'm leaving her, and I think she knows that.

I frown at the darkness of our bedroom.

This is cruel. I want to remember. I want to remember so bad.

Why has God does this to me?

———

I'm still sad lol

~Sam

Chapter Twenty Two:
Spokane

Chapter Twenty Two: Spokane

Alexander

I'm sitting at a table in a very crowded restaurant.

Rosie looks ill and I'm worried about her. Her skin is pale and she looks queasy. She's sweating even though it's February. I gently reach out and place a tender kiss against her cheek.

"You're sweating." I murmur. I reach out and remove her coat. She looks like she might throw up.

"I'm going to go to the restroom." She says softly. She stands up and crosses the restaurant.

She's so beautiful. I hope she's okay.

"I think she should go to the doctor." Mom says to me. "Alexander, she looks like she might have the stomach flu. She should go see a doctor."

"I know Mom." I reach for my phone and grab Rosie's on accident. The screen lights up and I glance down at it for a second, but the second is just long enough for me to see a message from some guy names Reagan.

Reagan: two questions. One, are you going to tell your husband about us? And two, are you going to tell him about the baby(ies)

I study the message for a second longer and then set her phone down.

It's not my business. I trust her with my life, because she is my life. She wouldn't do anything to hurt me. She wouldn't cheat on me.

But what baby? What is he talking about?

Since we got married our communication level has increased considerably.

"I'm going to go check on her." I say. I grab my phone and walk towards the bathroom, stopping outside. I lean against the wall and wait.

Ten minutes pass. Fifteen.

Right before the twenty minute mark, the door opens and my wife comes out. She still doesn't look well but she looks a bit better. Did she throw up?

Did she throw up because she's pregnant?

"Do you have a mint?" She asks when she sees me. She already knows that I do, so I reach into my pocket and drop it in her hand. She puts it in her mouth and watches me.

I might as well cut right to the chase. "I need to have a word with you." I say calmly.

"Okay..." she trails off.

"I wasn't trying to snoop, Rosie, but your phone lit up and I saw the messages." I hand her phone to her and watch as she reads them over. Her eyes widen slightly and she doesn't look up from the screen. I can see her hand tighten around her phone. "I'm not assuming anything." I say when she finally looks at me. "And I was not going through your phone. I trust you with my life. It lit up and I saw the message. I've never heard of a Reagan before."

She looks over her shoulder at our family watching us curiously. I can see her moving the mint around in her mouth. "Do you want to have this conversation now, or when we go back to the hotel?"

I hesitate. "On a scale of one to ten, ten being extremely serious, how serious is this?"

She watches me for a moment. "Three hundred." She says finally. "And no, I'm not cheating on you."

"I didn't think you were." I say. "We can wait until we're alone. Let's go back to the table. Our drinks are here and you look like you need some water."

I'm nearly positive she's pregnant and if she didn't cheat like she said she didn't, that means it's my baby.

She needs to drink and eat something. I watch when we get to the table as she sips her water, and when the waitress comes up and Rose declines food, I order what I know she was going to order anyways.

"She's going to get a chicken Cesar salad." I say. She looks at me and she opens her mouth to argue with me, but I just give her a look and she sighs, her shoulder slumping.

"Grilled chicken?" The waitress asks.

"Yes." I say simply.

A loud alarm rips me out of sleep and I sit up quickly. I hear a quiet, very annoyed groan next to me.

Who the fuck am I sleeping with?

Disoriented, I see Rose sleeping next to me.

Rose? The fucking teacher?

And then I remember she's my wife now and I don't remember her.

That dream felt so real, so, so real.

Reagan.

I hear her shut the alarm off, grumbling about being awake and packing.

"Who is Reagan?" I ask her.

"What?" She whines, half awake. She walks towards the bathroom but I follow her right into the bathroom.

"Who is Reagan?" I repeat.

"Reagan is my twin brother." She says.

Reagan is her twin brother.

But if her brother is Reagan, why didn't I know about him?

After deciding the dream is fake, I leave her alone to get dressed and I go upstairs to do the same.

As I stand in the shower, I know something is off.

That dream felt so real. It felt like a memory, not a dream. Last time I got a memory back, everything before it came back too, but this time all I have is the memory.

Was it real? It feels so real.

I knew she likes salad, grilled chicken Cesar.

My heart warms are the realization that I know I detail about her, even though it might be fake.

It's fake, Alex. Don't get your hopes up for no reason.

———

She got me and the twins and the dog in the car with suitcases packed. She dropped the dog off at a large two story house with a brick exterior, a white front door, and black window panels. Judging by the way she just walked in, I'm going to assume it's a family member.

She came back to the car and took us to the mall to get her new phone, and then we were at the airport, just barely catching a plane.

She wouldn't tell me where we were going but she sat with one of the twins in the car seat and I sat with the other one. We got the worst seats because it was a last minute flight but I'm not complaining.

I can't stop thinking about that dream.

Is it a dream or a memory? Usually dreams are hazy after you wake up and then they fade almost completely, but this one didn't. I remember everything about it.

The moment the plane touches the ground, I grab the car seat and stand up, lugging my son off the plane with me.

I wait by the gate and she meets me.

When I look around, I realize I know this airport. I've been to this airport.

But where is it?

Frustrated, I follow her to baggage.

I watch as she grabs all of our bags off the belt and gets a rental car.

We step outside into the snowy weather and I lug the car seats as she stacks the luggage and drags it.

"Do you know where we are?" She asks.

"We're in Spokane." I whisper.

"Yes." She says. "We're in Spokane."

She hits the button on the rental car and I load the twins in the car and then help her with the luggage.

As I load the luggage, I see her check the car seats to make sure they're buckled in properly.

I get in the car and she gets in the driver seat, turning the key in the engine.

"Are you ready?" She asks me.

"I guess." I mutter.

———

Vote and comment :(

~Sam

Chapter Twenty Three: Hippocampus

Chapter Twenty Three: Hippocampus

Rosabelle

All I've learned from this extensively painful experience with Alexander Caulton is that there at multiple different kinds of heartbreaks.

There's the most common kind, one where you lose a significant other. There's kind where you lose a best friend. The kind where you lose a pet. There's a kind where a family member dies.

But the most bitter, the most insufferably painful one, is the kind where you lose your significant other when neither one wants it.

I did everything I could. He let me push it to a month, and I took him anywhere I ever remembered going in Spokane. I got access to both of our old houses, and even Colton's. I took him to the high school we met at, stood him in the exact same spot. He already remembered that part but he doesn't remember anything.

I took him to California where he got Alice back and he remembered that. That memory came back, but I was hardly even in that memory, and he didn't remember the drive up. I took him to Dallas and got him to stand on the exact field that he won the Super Bowl on. I took him to the hotel where he found out I was pregnant. I took him to the mall in Milwaukee.

He didn't remember anything except for when he saw the message about Reagan on my phone.

And I know without a shadow of a doubt, that when we walk in the door tonight, he's going to pack.

He's going to pack up all of his things and he's going to leave, and I'm going to be alone to raise our kids.

And he doesn't know. He doesn't know me. He doesn't know.

I brought him to my parents house with the whole family and we tried to jog his memory but he just couldn't remember a thing. I too him to the gym, to his old house where he lived with Alice, I took him to the gym Alice goes to and the one I went to, I took him to the drive in theatre where we first messed around. I took him to the fair we went to for our first date, and the restaurant we went to.

I took him anywhere I could, even to my old house where we lost our virginity, where he found out about his mom.

I don't know what else to do. I don't know how else to help. He keeps telling me he's sorry and I just stopped answering him.

I know he's sorry. I'm sorry too.

That bitch that hit him...I'm going to sue her for all I have. I want her ass thrown in jail.

She ruined my entire life. My whole entire life.

Because he's my entire life, and he's gone.

She ruined my husband. She ruined me. She ruined our sons.

She ruined my happy ending.

I seriously didn't think this was the end, but now I'm nearly convinced.

I would make him fall back in love with me. I could do it easily, but he doesn't want to. He wants to start over.

"Where are we going now?" He whispers in the silence of the car.

"The hospital." I sniffle. I'm trying my best not to cry.

"Why?" He asks.

"You have a checkup appointment." I say dully.

"Okay."

"I'm sorry." He whispers. "I want to remember."

"I know." I say with a sigh. "It's not your fault."

We drive in complete silence from there.

I dropped the twins off at my parents' house.

The doctor looks sad for both of us as we sit in the room with him.

"Truthfully the scans are showing no reason for his memory to be lost. The temporal lobe controls memory and there's nothing there. The bleed wasn't even in the temporal lobe, so I have no idea why there would be memory loss."

"What if those tests aren't getting in far enough? Why can't you do a very detailed scan?"

"We could but it's very costly and it just might come up empty. Actually, I really think it will come up empty. Also, we don't have the equipment."

"But if you did." I say desperately. "If you had the equipment and you found there was a tumor o-or another bleed...that could be the cause?"

"Yes...it could be the cause."

There's something in his brain preventing him from remembering.

"Okay." I say. "Zane, let's go. Thank you for everything doctor."

"I hope everything works out, and I really am sorry."

Zane doesn't even say a word, he just walks out.

———

We went home and he went straight to the basement. I'm heartbroken and he's upset but I'm not giving up. He wouldn't give up on me and I'm not giving up on him. I'm not running.

So after frequent phone calls with the hospital Zane was in and hospitals around the country and having brain scans faxed, I made my decision.

I rented a private plane to Maryland.

I march down to the basement.

"We're going to Maryland."

"I'm not going anywhere else." He says. "I'm done Rose. I can't do it anymore. I can't."

He looks at me and there's tears in his eyes.

"it hurts. Everything fucking hurts. I want to remember and I can't. Sitting around with you and our sons is so fucking painful. I need to go. I'm moving back to California. You can take everything. Every fucking thing I have, I just need to go."

"You go with my to Maryland." I say. "And if I'm wrong and it doesn't work, I'll buy you a fucking mansion in California and you never have to think of me again."

"I don't want to. Why are you still fucking fighting for me? Why haven't you just given up?!"

"Because you would never give up on me. We don't give up on each other. You're the love of my life. You're my best friend. I'm not fucking giving up on you. We're going to fucking Maryland and the entire family is coming. We leave in three hours."

"I don't see the point-"

"You have everything to lose here." I say. "You have a family here. Friends. A career. A life. You made this life with me, and I know you're in there somewhere. I fucking refuse to throw you away and move on. I will not do it under any circumstance. You could beat the shit out of me and I would still come back. Please. Please, go with me to Maryland."

"We're going to Maryland and then I'm leaving. I can't fight any more. It hurts too much."

"I understand." I whisper. "If we go to Maryland and it doesn't work, I'll let you go."

"Just like that?" He whispers.

"You'll come back to me someday. We always come back to each other. Now come on, we're going to Maryland."

———

After making us sit around for nearly an entire day, the doctor comes strolling into the waiting room.

I feel like a bitch for praying for a tumor or a brain bleed that they can remove, but I can't help it.

He walks over to us with a small sigh.

News? Please tell me there's news.

Madison stands up with me but Zane stays seated. He done with me lugging him around the country. He's done seeing me getting my hopes up to have them crushed again.

He's done with me getting his hopes up and crushing them again.

"Well?" I ask.

I called the best neurosurgeon in the country in for this and he agreed claiming he was a fan of Zane's and of myself.

"You have a brain bleed in your hippocampus, which is in your temporal lobe." He says calmly. Zane stands up. "It's very small and nearly impossible to spot without very high tech machines. It's so small that it's going to be very difficult to remove and it's going to be a very long surgery. It's dangerous. Very dangerous, and if I mess up..." he clears his throat. "To be frank. If I mess up, I could wipe your memory completely. I could make you go blind. Deaf. I could sever your vocal chords. It's a high risk surgery and it will likely take over twelve hours, possibly twenty four. I could kill you."

"But you could do it right and I could be fine." Zane says.

"Yes." He says. "I've done a few of these surgery's successfully but it's important every one of you understands the risks."

"What if he doesn't get the surgery?" I ask.

"He'll likely never get his memory back but he'll live a healthy life. I'll leave you guys alone to discuss it."

"There's nothing to discuss. Do the surgery." Zane says.

"It could kill you." I say immediately. "And-"

"I don't care. I'm getting the surgery."

"But-"

"I'm getting the surgery." He repeats. "It's not a conversation. I'm walking around with a great life and a wife who loves me enough to die fighting for me, with a wife who loves me enough to let me go. I'm getting the surgery because I want to know my wife. I want to remember you. All of you. It's not fair. I'm getting the surgery."

I study him for a long time.

"You could die." I whisper.

"I'd rather die fighting than die knowing I did nothing to fix it."

"How do you know this is causing the memory loss?" Colton stands up.

"Because there is no other explanation." The doctor says. "And to be completely honest, it's their last hope."

Zane looks at me.

"Please Rose. Let me get the surgery."

Everyone is silent. Madison looks upset but she nods at me, almost thinking exactly what I'm thinking.

"Okay." I whisper. "You can get the surgery."

______

I am not a doctor please don't throw medical information at me

Okay bye

~Sam

Chapter Twenty Four: Surgery

Chapter Twenty Four: Surgery

The next morning we stand in Zane's hospital room. The doctors have him all ready for surgery and they're on their way up to take him.

I want to tell him I love him no matter what. I want to tell him if he wakes up without remembering anything I'll take care of him.

But I can't, because we have an audience.

After his parents and Alice say good bye and wish him luck, he looks at me.

"I'd like a moment alone with Rose please." He says.

He's very calm right now but I'm terrified.

Everyone hugs him goodbye and steps out into the hall.

"Come here." He whispers.

I take a deep breath and walk over to him. He opens his arms and pulls me down into a hug.

I let him hold me there for as long as he wants, and after a few minutes he pulls away.

"Listen," I begin. "I want you to know that if you wake up and you have no recollection of anything, not even your name, I'm still going to be here. I'll always be here. I'll always fight for you. Always." A tear rolls down my cheek and I wipe it on my sleeve. "And I want you to know if you wake up and you remember everything but you're blind...or deaf or mute...I'm still going to be here."

His eyes search mine for a long time.

"I love you." I whisper to him for the first time since I found out he doesn't know me. "And I'm sorry if that makes you uncomfortable, but I do. I really, really do, and everything is going to be fine. You're going to wake up with your memory back and you're going to heal and we'll go on to have all eight children. I promise."

"You can't promise me that." He smiles softly.

"I-I-" I stammer.

He takes my hand and holds it to his beating heart.

"If I don't come out of this alive...I need you to promise me you're going to move on. You're going to take your time to grieve and then move on. Please, please promise me you'll find happiness. I think me...that doesn't know me, and the me that does...I think we'd both want you happy. So promise me you'll move on."

"I can't promise that." I murmur. "But I promise I'll try as hard as I can. I promise I will."

He nods.

"I can accept that." He whispers. "Listen...before they take me I need you to know that even though I don't know you, I'm well aware how lucky I a m."

I smile at him and he reaches up to brush a tear off of my cheek.

"Everything is going to be fine, and if it's not, then you will be fine. Eventually." He swallows. "But make sure our kids don't grow up to be little assholes for me."

"Okay." I whisper.

He gently reaches up and pulls my lips down to his, kissing me for the second time in three months. It's a short kiss but it gets the seriousness across.

"Wish me luck?" He asks.

He doesn't know this, but he asked me that exact thing when we was going to win the Super Bowl.

So I say what I told him back them.

"I would..." I pause. "But you don't need it."

He smiles then and leans up to kiss my cheek.

"Alright. Let's get this over with."

———

Twenty four long grueling hours passed and a nurse or doctor would come in to tell us that he's still in surgery, but it was never his actual doctor.

I don't want the actual doctor until my husband is out of surgery.

My anxiety is through the roof and every member of the family is making sure I'm taken care of. They talk to me to distract me and I know they're struggling to keep the conversation going, but they're trying. Right now I'm resting with my head on Finn's shoulder.

I think Alice is really terrified so while everyone is trying to distract me, I'm trying to distract her and make sure she's okay. The twins are being taken care of by all of us and Alice is burying her feelings in them by playing with them and changing their diapers.

We're still waiting and the twins are sleeping in the stroller. It's eight in the morning and some of us are sleeping but I haven't fallen asleep.

Madison, James, and Alice haven't either. My head rets on Finn's shoulder and I'm staring at our babies sleeping.

God, I know I don't pray often but please let everything be okay. Let him wake up with his memories and no problems. I need a miracle here. Please.

Everyone has been trying to distract me and while I appreciate it, I'm starting to get annoyed.

The color my Mom is thinking of painting her kitchen is the last thing I want to hear about right now.

They took him yesterday morning and I feel overwhelmed.

I want reality. I want to discuss my feelings, but the only person I usually discuss them with might wake up and he might never be the same.

He might not wake up at all. That's the reality.

And I'm scared shitless.

And memories, memories that have been wiped from his brain since December are crippling me.

I need him to be okay. I need him to be okay for me.

"You know?" Alice breaks the silence. "The fact that the doctor hasn't come in yet is good."

How is that good? All of us give her weird looks so she explains.

"If the doctor isn't here, it means he's with Zane, which means he's still alive."

That's true. That's very true.

"Also..." she clears her throat. "If things don't work out with this surgery, I'm moving in with Rose."

"What?" Madison asks.

"I'm moving in with Rose. She needs somebody. I can be her person. We can help each other."

"Nothing is going to go wrong." James says confidently. "Look, here comes Doctor Ries."

We all look up to see Zane's doctor walking into the waiting room.

Everyone that's sleeping is jerked awake and we're all on our feet. I clasp my hands together and press them against my mouth.

Please give me good news.

Please. Please give me good news. Please. Please.

"The reason it took so long is because before we put him out, he asked us to not come to you guys with any news until we knew for sure because he didn't want to give anybody false hope." He says. "And he was rather insistent."

Okay, I don't give a shit about that. Is he okay?

"His memory is still something we don't know about because he's groggy." He pauses. "But he's awake. He's responsive, he can see and talk and hear, and he told us to come get you guys...so he at least knows you're all here, so he must have some memory."

"Well lets go find out." Alice says. She starts pushing the stroller towards the elevator and I follow her.

We take two different elevators to the ICU and we pause outside of Zane's hospital room.

Everyone looks at me expectantly.

They want me to go first.

"I-" I clear my throat. "I can't go first."

"You're going first." Vanessa says. "Go." She nudges me towards the door.

"Let's go together." I say.

They all nod in agreement. I wipe my hands off on my jeans and grip the cold metallic handle.

"Please keep in mind that he's on drugs. The anesthesia wore off already but he's on pain meds. The medicine could make his memory groggy so if he doesn't know who everyone is right away, don't be alarmed. The memory could come back gradually now. If he doesn't know everything right away, it doesn't mean he won't eventually know."

I nod at the doctor and open the door quietly.

"Why not?" I hear him ask. I push the door open wider and see he's talking to a male nurse.

"Because you just had surgery.

"It's across the street though. I'll pay for it. You can get whatever you want, just make sure they give me two McDouble's and not one, because last time I asked for two they switched it to a meal and I didn't get my second burger." He says. "Look, I'll give you some cash. You get some food for yourself. Fuck, feel the whole hospital if you want."

He doesn't seem like he's confused. He seems...normal. My heart is pounding in my chest and I'm worried I might go into cardiac arrest. He glances up when we all walk in, watching as we each enter. He studies all of our faces intently and then raises his right hand, wiggling his fingers in a wave.

"Alexander, this is your family." Dr. Ries says.

Zane glances at all of us and then turns back to the nurse.

"So what do you say?"

"You can't have McDonald's." The nurse laughs.

"Whatever. I'll have somebody sneak it in. There are a lot of people in here. I'm sure somebody will sneak me in some McDonald's.

"You can have McDonald's when you get discharged." Dr. Ries says.

He gives up and we fall into silence. He stares at his hands, tracing the lines on his palm.

I'm not sure what to do. I don't want to approach him and overwhelm him.

"Do you remember?" Alice finally asks.

His eyes snap up to his little sisters and then flicker to me and back to Alice.

I know the answer before he says it.

He doesn't remember.

"I remember the accident." He says. "I remember getting hit and getting out and getting hit by a car. I know the car was blue and it was a sedan, I think a Hyundai." He swallows."And I remember everything from when I woke up until...whenever I went into surgery. I know I got memories back I but lost them again."

So the tiny little recollection he had of me is gone.

It's gone. He doesn't remember me at all.

He looks at me.

"I'm sorry." He says.

Chapter Twenty Five: Signature

C hapter Twenty Five: Signature

I left. I took the twins and walked out. I went to the hotel and I cried myself to sleep. I woke up when the twins did and was up the whole time they were and slept when they were sleeping. I couldn't move. It hurt.

I forced myself to put them in the bath. I took a shower when they were sleeping.

I got dressed and I forced myself to go back to the hospital.

Now, for the first time ever, my hope is gone. It's been three days.

I push the stroller down the hallway, nearly crashing into my twin on the way. He grabs my arm.

"Are you okay?" He asks.

"How is he?" I whisper.

"He's...he feels really guilty." He says. "And he keeps asking if you're okay."

If I can't have the man I married, I'll teach him. I'll make him fall back in love with me.

I won't give up on him. Never.

Never.

"I'm going in to see him." I say.

"I'll come with you." He says.

Nodding, we walk together to his hospital room.

Before I go in, Reagan turns to me.

"Bella, you should know that Dr. Ries said-"

But I was already stepping in the room when he said it so his voice cuts off.

I walk into the room at the way and see Zane sitting up in bed scrolling through his phone.

Everyone looks up when I walk in. All side conversations end.

"You came back." Zane says, slowly setting his phone down.

"Yeah."

Something is going to happen.

Even this version of Zane I know. I know the old Zane's facial expression. At least he kept that.

Before he has a chance to say what he's going to tell me, I speak.

"You're filing for divorce."

His eyes study me for a moment.

"Yeah." He whispers.

I stuff my hands in the pockets of my sweatshirt.

I don't cry. I don't flip out. I don't tell him I'm going to keep fighting.

There's nothing left to fight for. He knows it and so do I.

I don't say anything, so he continues. "I want to remember you, Rose." He whispers. "I do. I want to remember so bad. It kills me." He swallows. "But I just...I just don't. I'm sorry.

I want to cuss him out. I want to tell him I fucking hate him.

"And the doctor said that if I don't remember yet, I probably never will."

But I can't. I don't hate him. I love him. I love him so much that I'm going to let him leave. He deserves to be happy.

"Please say something." He whispers.

I can't find my voice, so I gesture to the stroller where the twins are.

"I don't..." he trails off.

"You don't want them." I whisper.

"I want them." He says. "But I can't. I just...can't. I don't remember anything, Rose. In my mind, I'm a virgin. In my mind, there's no way they're m ine."

"But they are yours." I say, and a tear rolls down my cheek.

I'm so fucking tired of crying. I'm so sick of it. I wipe it away angrily and fold my arms across my chest.

"I know." He looks pained. "But I don't remember. They're just babies. They're not my babies. Not to me."

This is so fucking unfair.

I hate everything. I hate the world. I hate the fucking bitch that hit him with her car. I hate my life. I hate it. I hate everything.

"You can have everything." He continues. "I just want the truck."

This isn't real. This isn't fucking real.

I want to bash my head against a wall.

"And money..."

He has the papers in front of him. He already got the papers.

Why can't he just remember? Why the hell can't he just remember?

If I step forward and sign those papers...that's it.

"I won't take a lot of money." He says. "I-"

"You can take as much money as you want."

Silence.

He wants me to sign.

He's waiting for me to sign.

Just sign and run. Sign and run.

I cross the room and grab the pen.

"Where do I sign?"

My voice if flat and void of any emotion.

He points to the right spot and I look directly into his eyes.

But there's no change. He doesn't remember.

So I press the pen to the paper and I sign, and then I drop the pen into his hand.

It felt like it weighed a million pounds when it was just a few ounces.

"Promise me something." He whispers. I just nod. "If the twins see pictures of me...of us..." he swallows. "Please tell them the truth."

I just nod again.

"Promise."

He scribbles his signature on the other line and I hear a few sniffles around the room.

I stare at the two signatures, and the realization hits me.

I'm divorced. We're divorced.

We got divorced.

I'm single.

I feel like the walls are closing in on me. I need to get the fuck out of here and I need to do it now.

So I run. I grab the twins and I run as hard as I can, taking the elevator to the first floor. I run out of the hospital and I just keep running until I stop next to some alley and throw up. The twins are crying and I feel like the world is crashing down around me.

I need to get the fuck out of here.

I need to go.

www.ingramcontent.com/pod-product-compliance
Lightning Source LLC
Chambersburg PA
CBHW070600170726
48291CB00003B/648